ACTS OF FAITH

ACTS OF FAITH

Hans Koning

A Donald Hutter Book

Henry Holt and Company

New York

First published in the United States in 1988 by
Henry Holt and Company, Inc., 115 West 18th Street,
New York, New York 10011.
Published in Canada by Fitzhenry & Whiteside Limited,
195 Allstate Parkway, Markham, Ontario L3R 4T8.

Library of Congress Cataloging-in-Publication Data
Koning, Hans, 1921–
Acts of faith / by Hans Koning. —1st American ed.
p.   cm.
Reprint. Originally published: London : Gollancz, 1986.
ISBN 0-8050-0677-X
I. Title.
PS3561.046A64   1988
813'.54—dc19   87-26338
                                                      CIP
First American Edition
Printed in the United States of America
10 9 8 7 6 5 4 3 2 1

The characters in this novel are fictional. No real
persons are portrayed and, specifically, no real
employees of the New York Public Library, the
Miami police, or the FBI.

An excerpt from this novel appeared in *The Paris
Review* in the fall of 1987.

ISBN 0-8050-0677-X

To Kate

The author expresses his thanks to the National
Endowment for the Arts in Washington, D.C., for their
help in keeping him alive as a novelist.

ACTS OF FAITH

I

When the visitor walked into the coffeehouse on the central square of Pamplona, he saw with some pleasure that nothing had changed. Vast, dark, almost empty, it looked just as it had on his first Spanish visit ten years before. He even remembered the old man who was leafing through the café newspapers in their wooden holders as if he had been doing nothing else all that time in between. The same waiter in the continental-style long white apron was polishing the same coffee urn.

Ten years earlier, 1973, he had driven into Pamplona on a dark February afternoon under a slashing rain. The square had been empty, he had left his rented car between the columns of ochre stone and ducked into the coffeehouse, to warm himself—near a pot-bellied stove? No, surely near a radiator even then.

Now, the late summer of 1983, so many cars had been parked in the square every which way, Volkswagens with German plates, Renaults from Paris right on the sidewalk, that he had had to continue to a parking lot quite a distance off. He had walked back through throngs of people, tourists with children holding balloons of the Pamplona fair, and chewing on the famous sausages which the local stores pyramid in their windows in their multicolored wrappers with signs, We Ship Everywhere. A number of the giftshops and foodshops had the same bullfight poster for a background.

'22 Junio 1941', surprisingly, the date on the poster said.

The air was very warm and heavy with car fumes, but inside the cavernous coffeehouse it felt cool. The waiter, when he brought the order, let his eyes rest on his customer's face longer than normal. Perhaps he had a sudden recollection of a decade ago when he had served that same man, sitting at that same table, through a series of gloomy February afternoons? Various locals used to share his table then, explaining to the visitor life under Franco and the Pamplona trial of the three Basque terrorists, or separatists as one man had dared

7

call them after a quick glance over the sea of chairs, the old billiard tables in an unlit corner.

Perhaps when the visitor paid, the waiter would remark on that past and ask his customer why he had reappeared.

For no special reason, the visitor would answer. Please don't think I was or am involved in the Basque problem or any other such problem, he'd say, I came here ten years ago only because they sent me. (Very moderate) expenses paid.

II

That visitor's name was John Balthasar, of West 104th Street in Manhattan. He had arrived in Pamplona this time, summer 1983 that is, from the south of France where he had been on vacation with his girlfriend Diana. A vacation which had started well but which had collapsed when Diana's mother started calling from America, to say that Diana's husband kept pestering her to find out where his wife was—although they had been separated for a year—and would Diana please do something about him. After a hundred dollars' worth of telephone conversations with the husband, Diana had agreed to come to New York and had left John Balthasar by himself.

Focusing more on his surroundings, Balthasar now found the south of France not that marvelous. Presumably it was different in the old days, he had thought, when it looked as in those paintings by Bonnard. He had got bored and restless and very frustrated trying not to stare at near-naked girls and women. Contrary to what he had thought when Diana was still with him, it wasn't easy to pick up a girl there, not when you were approaching forty and drove around in a little Renault-4 with a Hertz sticker. All he could find were hookers. He had decided to go to Spain.

When he had announced that to the Hertz clerk, the man had started talking about Pamplona and its fairs. Balthasar had planned to visit Barcelona. He hated fairs and the sort of crowds that go with them. He was a man who longed for eighteenth century travel or eighteenth century travel as he imagined it, with inns lost in an empty landscape, a stagecoach lurching through the night, a mysterious young woman next to you, a vast world in which distance itself was an adventure. None the less, he had driven to Pamplona.

There was no need to explain his reappearance ten years later to the Pamplona coffeehouse waiter. The man silently handed him his check and swept the money off the table into the pocket of his apron.

Outside it had cooled off but it was as packed as before in the square. John Balthasar hastened away from it and at each corner he chose the quieter street, until he found himself in a residential neighborhood walking between two rows of well-to-do houses, with wrought-iron balconies, heavily curtained windows, and no signs of human life. Flocks of sparrows or some such birds in the front gardens took off without a sound as he approached and settled down behind him. New York sparrows make a lot of noise, he thought. To these mute creatures there was an unnerving connotation. They made him think of a dream. The dream told to Joseph in the Bible by his fellow prisoner who will be hanged.

Perhaps fear of birds went back to a memory, back to when we used to see them pick out the eyes of the hanged on the gallows. Perhaps fears of nature were enmeshed with human acts, guilt. He vaguely felt he had got hold of a new notion there.

It hadn't been the car rental man with his fairs who had made him come to Pamplona. A regret connected with that town had been pulling at him during those years between his two visits. Balthasar tended to be a regretter, a man pursued by an ever lengthening string of deplored recollections; he still regretted the flip answer he had given his gradeschool teacher—he must have been six or seven—when she asked him if he knew the names of the parents of Jesus.

A ten year old regret had brought him back.

III

Pamplona, February 1973. In those days John Balthasar was a freelance journalist living in London, which was cheap; his top-floor apartment in a nice house in Hampstead, rent-controlled, cost him a thousand dollars a year. He had been doing some articles for *Penthouse*, not the New York one but the British edition. ('Less money but less pubic hair,' was the office joke). The winter in London had been miserable and when the editor phoned one day and asked, "How's your Spanish?", Balthasar without hesitation answered, "Fine." It was the kind of thing you could fake, he felt, and there had been talk about a big feature on the American and German millionaires who were busy buying up the Spanish coasts.

That wasn't what the editor wanted from him, though. He needed four thousand words on the Basques and the Basque terrorist trial going on in Pamplona. The Basques demanded autonomy and were throwing bombs at the Franco police; in England as in the US the magazine ran those social consciousness articles to offset the girlie pages. A thousand dollars and very moderate expenses, the editor told Balthasar.

"And what about the Costa Brava millionaires?" Balthasar asked.

"That one has been given out in New York, to Marjorie Hutchings. She was the runner-up for the Pulitzer Prize three years ago."

"Well, wow."

"Take the Aviola flight London–Bordeaux," the editor said. "They give us a discount."

In that way Balthasar had ended up his first time, in the year 1973, in Pamplona, where the month of February turned out to be as gray and cold and wet as London had been.

He managed the assignment all right. It was not too difficult to find people willing to talk to an American journalist. After Pamplona, he spent some days in San Sebastian, and then returned to Pamplona. Of the journalists he had met there, he had become friendly with one, an elderly man who wrote about literature while slipping in words of encouragement, or so he told Balthasar, to the cause of the Basque language. (The Basques have their own language but under Franco were forbidden to use it). That man's name was Miguel Ruiz. He had a big, bald head under his beret, and they sat for hours in the coffeehouse, Miguel sipping from a tumbler of brandy which in Spain then was cheaper than Coca-Cola, Balthasar drinking endless coffees.

10

Balthasar's last morning, when he had come in to say goodbye to Miguel, a young girl of eighteen or even younger, sat at their table. She shook hands with Balthasar. Miguel said she had come to ask him a favor and he would translate.

There was a lot of whispering between Miguel and the girl and then Balthasar was told that her fiancé had to visit someone in France, and could he give him a lift to wherever he was going himself?

"To Bordeaux," he said. "That's where I rented my car. Sure. Why not."

"I'm just translating," Miguel said slowly. "I am not telling you, you must do this."

"It's all right." Balthasar realized the boy was probably in some kind of trouble. An American passport carried a lot of weight, though, with Franco officials.

The girl whispered some more.

"What?" Balthasar asked.

"Nothing. She worries too much."

The girl had been pretty. No, more than pretty, a pale, a chiseled face. As of a nymph on a Roman fountain, he thought. She was wearing a hooded cape which showed a lock of hair, not black like most girls in that town, but reddish. Hyacinth colored. Thy hyacinth hair, thy classic face. He could never fall short of such a girl's expectations.

Miguel continued, "He has no passport but he must have a border-crossing card of course. She asks, what kind of car do you have?"

"He'll be comfortable enough."

"No. She asks."

"An Opel. An ugly big black thing. It's all they had at the Bordeaux airport."

The girl nodded as Miguel translated.

Balthasar had expected a boy her age, and it was a bit of a shock when the following morning at seven the fiancé showed up at his hotel and turned out to be a man older than Balthasar, a hefty fellow in boots and a camouflage army jacket with bulging pockets. He nodded at Balthasar, shook hands silently, and got in the car.

In his hitchhiking days Balthasar had always felt obliged to offer conversation to the driver, but this man stared ahead and when Balthasar said something about the misery of the never-ending rain, he only made a sound of assent. After that they drove in silence through a landscape gradually widening in the morning light.

Balthasar chose the shortest route out, straight to Bayonne, the way he had come, over the Puerto de Velate pass. At the top of the pass he stopped the car.

"I need a quick look around," he explained to his passenger. He had decided to start his article with the pass, with him standing there two thousand feet above the valley and looking down on the old invasion route into the plain, above him the Velate fortress which used to guard that passage and in his mind's eye the many armies that had struggled through here, Napoleon's, the Carlists, the miserable legions of the defeated from so many civil wars. (The magazine ran the article, but with all this cut out.)

Balthasar did not stay outside the car long. It was bitterly cold. The fortress turned out to be but a ruin. In the distance he could make out two farmhouses built of rough stone, but nothing stirred near them. On their way up the rain had stopped, but now wet snow flakes started to fall, very slowly and far apart. Along the horizon were streaks of blue sky and as they began the drive downhill, a bundle of sunlight, separate rays, appeared between two mountain tops. The rays picked out each falling snow flake. Balthasar shivered.

"Sun and snow," his passenger suddenly said in accentless English. "What they call here, the Devil's Fair."

The left shoulder of the road followed the mountainside, and to the right it fell away steeply toward the valley. Balthasar didn't remember this from his drive in. The steering felt slippery but there was no other traffic at all. Far below he saw a village and then a zigzagging sideroad leading down to it. A sign said, Maya, 1 kilometer.

"I better hide now," his passenger said with a little smile.

"Hide?"

"In the trunk. You did agree to that?"

Balthasar stopped the car on the left side of the road, close to the mountain slope. "Well, no."

12

A silence.

"Miguel said you had a border-crossing card," Balthasar muttered.

His passenger shook his head without explaining.

"What would happen if they find you in there?"

A grimace.

"What would happen to me?" Balthasar asked.

His passenger shook his head again. He looked completely unconcerned. "Miguel is an idiot," he announced. "He always overestimates people." Then he opened his door and got out. "Adiós," he said, and started walking back up the road.

Balthasar rolled his window down and stuck out his head, but he could not see the man because of the mountain which rose almost vertically beside him. He started to back up, but clumsily hit the slope with his rear bumper. He stopped again. What shall I do? That man going off rather than even trying to argue with a half-assed American. He moved over on the seat to the right and opened the door. "Wait!" he called out.

The sun had vanished, the snow was coming down thickly. He saw his passenger quite far off but he had been heard, for the man stood still and then started walking toward the car. That little smile seemed to be back on his face.

Balthasar blinked against the snow hitting his eyes on a gust of wind. Images of men kicking you, prison cells, vomit, excrement. Nothing he had ever experienced. Images from war movies, perhaps. The clean courage of men in movies.

I will never see these people again.

He slid back behind the wheel, without looking, without even closing the right-hand door first, and drove off.

IV

That was all.

The name Pamplona. In the following years, until Franco died and even afterward, there was every so often a little item on some inside page of *The New York Times* about Basques condemned to death by the Madrid government. They still executed people in

13

Spain by strangling them with an iron collar, he thought. Perhaps it was not any worse than gas or injections; you can't put a man down painlessly like a dog. The pain is in the knowing.

There is a group of wax figures in Morro Castle near Havana, which he had once visited. It shows the garrote in action, the choking victim purple-faced, his eyes bulging, and a very pale priest holding out a little silver cross to the man. (To remind him—of what? Mercy? Love?)

Now, ten years later, he was walking a silent Pamplona street, sparrows rising in front of him. He came to a little park and sat down on a bench. The sky was darkening to purple. A convertible drove by with the top down, leaving a wake of rock music. He told himself he was actually glad he had never found out what had happened to his passenger of the year 1973.

Of course, if, after all, he did want to know, it should be possible. Ten years is not that long to follow back through time. Although Miguel had already been an old man in 1973; chances were he was no longer alive.

He got up from his bench and started walking again. Ahead of him the character of the street was changing; electrical signs were coloring the twilight. He passed restaurants and bars, serious places with potted palm trees in the entrances, one with a bust of an old king of Spain or perhaps it was Nero or Cervantes, and liveried doormen. Then on the next corner a McDonald's was blinking at all this formality. He went in there to eat.

When he came back out on to the street, he discovered a telephone booth, painted a shiny new white, the first one he had seen in Pamplona; it even turned out to hold a directory. Impossible to walk on. He looked up Miguel's newspaper, the *Diario de Navarra*, he had the change in his hand and dialed the number. "Miguel Ruiz, the editore literaria," he asked. It sounded wrong to him but the girl seemed to understand. Then a man came on who said something sharply. "Qué?" Balthasar shouted, feeling the man was going to hang up. "No such person here," the man told him in English.

A woman was waiting outside the phone booth and he smiled happily at her as he opened its door. He experienced a very strong

14

sense of relief. He had been lucky; he had been playing with fire. No harm had been done.

He showed her the ticket of the parking lot where he had left the little Renault and she pointed out the direction for him. It was not far. In the early evening he drove off toward Madrid, where he had never been and which was less than two hundred miles away.

His predilection for small roads got him lost. He thought he could get to Madrid driving more or less parallel to the autopista, the turnpike, but as night fell the towns he passed through became smaller and smaller and the name Madrid disappeared from the road signs. He did not mind. He was just messing around anyway.

Harm had after all been done by that phone call, though. The words of that embryonic conversation kept running through his mind, he couldn't get rid of them. Making that call had been imprudent.

The dark landscape remained invisible. The road was delineated by gas stations and big open-air lots where car tires were stacked up in huge numbers but without a soul present; behind their bright vapor lights he distinguished only a shadowy haze.

But every now and again he caught a glimpse of a lamp-lit room in a farmhouse, with a woman cooking or children sitting around a table. People who knew where their home was, where the center of their world was. He envied them with a near desperate intensity. Then there was nothing except the darker silhouette of mountains against the sky, and the white line of the road racing toward him in the headlights.

The car radio played an opera from a middle European German-language concert hall. His thoughts and senses were all in different places.

V

Very late he came through a small town and when he saw the neon sign of a hotel he stopped and went in.

Once past the lobby, the place was shabbier than he had expected, but it was cheap. He climbed up to the top floor (the man at

15

the desk had given him the key and just pointed at the ceiling) and followed a long, dim corridor to his room. The room was pitch-dark, its shutters closed, and it took him a while to locate the light switch. A twenty-five watt bulb in a tulip-shaped glass lamp showed a bed on high legs, a chair, a bit of red carpet, a wash basin, and on the wall, a Heart of Jesus shedding blood and tears.

The sheets on the bed were clean and he tossed his clothes on the chair, climbed into bed and turned off the lamp. He had meant to do some thinking, reach some conclusions about his girl friend's desertion, about Miguel, about his life—but now, lying in the absolute darkness of the hotel room, he was in a vacuum of emotions.

All he experienced was frustration, at being in a foreign country without a woman.

When he opened his eyes, harsh white light came in through the chinks in the shutters. It was hot. Pushing the shutters out, he discovered that his room looked down on a large cobbled square without a single tree, lying empty and already baking in the sun; the night before he had come in from a narrow street at the back. He could not find a toilet on his floor and after peeing in the wash basin, shaving, and giving himself a stand-up bath, he packed up. He paid the woman behind the desk and came out into the street to find that the car, left at the entrance, had vanished.

"The police take your car," the reception lady said.

"But why didn't you call me? How stupid!"

"I do not know. They do not ask," she said angrily. "It blocks the street."

"Blocks what? The town dog?"

She telephoned, talked at length, and then told him, "The fine is ten thousand pesetas."

That was close to a hundred dollars. "Tell them to go to hell," he said.

She spoke some more on the telephone and hung up.

"Well, what?"

"Nothing."

So he had the way to the police station pointed out to him. Soon he could see it at the top of a steeply climbing avenue, a white building of large stone blocks looking like a Foreign Legion barracks, and he slowly made it up the hill in the shadow of the trees,

16

shifting his bag from one hand to the other. Two Guardia Civil men, a kind of militia, surly and tough looking, stood at the entrance. They showed him into an office where a policeman waved him into a chair and offered him a cigaret. Balthasar shook his head and then thought, it doesn't take any guts making a scene in a little police station here when you're an American tourist, and he accepted the cigaret.

"Your car?" the police officer said.

"Yes. I—"

"Perhaps we can forgive the fine."

Did the man want a bribe? Ten dollars would be better than a hundred but you had to be sure or you made it worse. It did not seem in character: the officer was quite dashing in his appearance. His office was seedy, though. A worn carpet on a cement floor; walls of crumbling plaster. They were papered with notices and announcements, some half covering others, a few so old they had turned yellow. On the wall behind the desk hung a bullfight poster and it was another one of those he had seen in Pamplona: the matador about to shake his sword free of his cape and plunge it into the bleeding bull. That date: 22 Junio 1941.

The police officer asked, "My poster—do you like it?"

"It's beautifully drawn. It could be a Goya."

The officer looked pleased.

"I've seen them in Pamplona. Why are there so many of them around, since they're forty years old? Yours looks new, actually."

"We reprint them," the man answered. He studied Balthasar's face and started writing something on a slip of paper. "Here. Your car is in the courtyard."

As he now appeared to expect neither a hundred nor ten dollars, Balthasar stood up. "Thank you, inspector."

The leg of his chair had caught on the carpet's edge, and while he walked around it with his bag, he noticed a row of Wanted notices near the door, the kind displayed in American post offices. He took a step toward them.

"We like to take stock of our visitors. It was good of you, to come here," the policeman said.

"Well, I didn't have much—" Some of the Wanted notices were recent but others were faded and tattered. And there in the middle of the row he saw a face he knew, a man with a fierce look and a thick mustache. The picture was spotted by moisture and the effect was somewhat as if the man had been photographed standing in a snow storm. He was Balthasar's passenger of 1973.

John Balthasar stopped. Was he imagining things? He felt dizzy —how could it happen that—He searched for a date on the notice and started to try and translate the text.

But the police chief had opened the door of his office with one hand and with the other took Balthasar by the arm and half-steered, half-pulled him along. "You have to hurry. At noon the gates are locked till four o'clock. Have a good voyage."

VI

In the courtyard Balthasar gave the slip of paper to a Guardia Civil who walked him to his car. Various forms were stuck under the windshield wiper. The man removed them, opened the door for him and saluted.

Balthasar lowered his car windows and sat motionless. He had to pull himself together, shake off a sense of unreality. At the gate a man stood, beckoning him to get out, waiting to lock up.

Down the avenue at great speed, and at the bottom he noticed a blue arrow pointing to the right for Madrid—just in time, for it was a sharp turn and the little car lurched around it. A series of curves followed, a straight road through a bare and featureless plain, and then he found himself on a major highway going south. Here the traffic was heavy but it kept moving at speed.

A couple of hours later he saw in the far distance the church spires of Madrid glow in the low sun, with far to the southwest the hazy mountains of Guadarrama at the horizon.

That was a sentence from a book, a 1910 travel memoir he had bought on Fourth Avenue for five dollars, the only book he had read to prepare himself for his first journey to Spain, the *Penthouse* one. Those words had stayed with him and he repeated them now, "In the far distance the church spires of Madrid glow in the low sun, with far to the southwest the hazy mountains of Guadarrama."

But what happened to him was only that the fast-flowing traffic started to congeal; the cars crawled from stoplight to stoplight and that was how he knew he was approaching Madrid. All he saw was service stations and shacks, bare lots strewn with papers and bottles, poor and dirty children, and signs saying, To the Airport.

Then the traffic crept past dry fountains, parks, and fat government buildings with the red and yellow flag of the country. He sat at a stoplight, beside a building marked, "Post—Telephone—Telegraph", and when a car pulled out ahead of him, he parked at its meter and went in. He was going to phone his girlfriend Diana.

He wasn't sure why. The entry into Madrid had disheartened him. Five o'clock, late morning in New York. She answered on the second ring, and did not sound surprised to hear his voice; when he asked in a monotone, "And will we see each other when I get back?", she said, "Of course. I'm sorry. I've been very silly."

That was easy, too easy perhaps. Still, it cheered him up, not because he had been jealous but because it freed of him of the weight of being lost, of not belonging anywhere. When he came down the wide stone steps of the post office and looked out over the avenue with its honking cars and arguing pedestrians, the scene did not seem inimical any more but inviting. He longed now to immerse himself in this distant capital.

Late that evening he was wandering through little streets of shabby bars and nightclubs.

He had left his jacket and tie with his bag in a hotel. He did not want to look like a tourist or indeed like himself; he would have wanted to blend in with the drunks standing in doorways of bars and the aggressive looking men sauntering down the middle of the street. The lightheartedness following his phone call to Diana had gone. Why he wished to *belong*, in the slum neighborhood of a foreign city he had never been in before, he did not know. It wasn't that he was romanticizing Madrid or Spain. He did not admire that cruel and tormented race.

He thought, no outsider can understand this reality, can touch it. Only through a woman. Touch—precisely, literally. By touching her body. Or the same for a woman, through a man. The only bridge.

19

But there were no women unaccompanied by men in those streets.

Then, peering past a bead curtain, he saw a young woman sitting by herself at a bar, her legs crossed, an empty glass in front of her. He went in and sat down on the next stool, ordered a brandy and looked at her with a gesture toward her empty glass. She ordered a drink too and smiled at him, a rather horrible smile because she lacked several front teeth. But she had a gentle face, somber, and a slim body in a yellow dress on which thin and pointed red flames were depicted. She made a movement with her head toward the door, and said, "Twenty dollars." Streetwalkers, oil, arms, all get quoted in dollars.

"Ten," Balthasar suggested, for he had very little money left now to last him until his charter flight back to the States.

"Eighteen."

"Oh, okay."

They climbed the stairs in a house a few doors from the bar, she entered a room and sat down on a daybed. She asked in English, "You want the mouth, or the belly? The mouth is ten dollars more."

He answered, "Just do it with your hands," because it was filthy in there and on the way they had passed a pharmacy with a display of bottles and a sign saying only, Sifilis. But then he thought that the woman looked offended and he said, "Well, no. The other thing. Belly."

"Undressing is five dollars more."

"Okay, okay."

She hung her clothes over a chair beside the daybed. Her body was dark and muscular and he now saw that she was younger than he had realized in the bar. He lay on her, looking away from her mouth with the missing teeth, staring instead at the red and yellow of her dress hanging beside his head and at her hair which was dyed black, with reddish roots. With her every move, the daybed creaked as if in pain. How cool her body feels, he thought, the body of this Madrid girl, this stranger who suddenly—An overwhelming wave of lust swept over him, he dug his fingers into her shoulders and came with a violent shudder.

VII

Back out on the street.

He decided to return to his hotel, have a wash, go to sleep. But when he passed that same bar, he entered. A moment later the yellow-dress girl came in too but she did not look at him. That was the etiquette of her profession, he thought.

Here I am, alone, staring at the hands of a barman with black nails, white shirtsleeves with red stripes, ducking the dirty glasses into an overflowing sink. So much for making yourself belong through a woman.

Still, if I sat next to her again, if we started to talk. First I'd explain to her, I'm not one of those tourist types who imagine there's something to sentimentalize about a miserable business transaction. This is different, I would say, there is something connected with you, I would say, a memory. I have never seen you before but there are recognitions—Oh balls, she'd say, or the Spanish equivalent.

A man walked in and went up to her and she handed him some money without saying a word; his money, Balthasar assumed. The man gave her a pat on her behind and left. He hadn't been as Balthasar would have expected, no sharp-faced fellow with oily black hair and a soft tread, but a lumbering sort with a dirty blond fringe and pale eyes. More like a German farmer than a Madrid pimp. The girl followed him with her eyes as he left; Balthasar tried to make her look his way but she remained staring at the swaying bead curtain. Balthasar got up, walked past her, and set out for his hotel. He had its address on a card; it turned out to be near. He had been meandering in narrow circles.

But once up in his room and about to unpack his bag, the realization struck him that he did not want to be there and that there was no point in being there. Why spend money to sleep in that dark anonymous room which had absorbed the fears and expectations of ten thousand lonely men, why wake up in one more anonymous dawn? Why see more of the capital of an alien country whose twenty or thirty or forty millions, he did not know how many, did not touch his life or his death at any point? He stuffed his jacket and tie into his bag, draped his raincoat over it (he had not paid yet), and carried it downstairs and through the lobby without anyone stopping him. He got his car back from a half-awake attendant in the parking lot who pointed out the direction for getting out of town, going north.

It was half past one in the morning then and a cool breeze blew through the car. He felt better. As long as I keep moving, he thought.

When Madrid was behind him, he stopped to buy gas at an all-night station bathing in fluorescent light. It was straddling an intersection; when he turned northeast afterward, the man at the pumps whistled so sharply on his fingers that he heard him over the engine and stopped. The attendant pointed with one finger toward the highway north, to show that was the direction for France. Balthasar waved to thank him but continued northeast, on a narrow road.

Torrelaguna, it said on a metal sign so small and so high up a pole that it might have been for coaches or horsemen once, and after that there were no more road signs, no billboards, only fields, glittering little lakes, and every now and again a lightless farmhouse, all clearly visible in a late risen sickle moon. The road twisted and turned and he had to be careful. At times he lost the moon but then it reappeared over a ridge or between tall trees, at his right but behind him, showing he was still heading northeast. It was a pleasant idea, to travel steered by the moon.

Much later he was startled by the sound of the car engine knocking sharply and the car slowing down. He realized he was going up a steep hill and had been about to fall asleep, and at the top of the climb he pulled over on to the grass of an open space. When he switched off the headlights, he found himself in total night. The moon had set, the one sound was of the wind in the tree tops. He turned up the windows and stretched out on the seat as best as he could.

He tried all sorts of positions, even letting his legs stick out of the door. He was glad when morning broke, a sunless foggy morning which slowly revealed the plain far below. He walked around in the grass, chewing on a stick of brittle gum he had found at the back of the glove compartment.

When the light became stronger and his horizon opened up, he discovered a small town in the distance, clusters of houses and trees, and he realized that he was, unaccountably, looking at the town of the police station with that Wanted bulletin for his passenger on its wall. He could clearly distinguish that steep avenue and the barracks it led up to.

Afterwards he did not remember having been surprised by this. He was preoccupied by a malaise, a gigantic unease, begun, it seemed, by his Pamplona telephone call to Miguel Ruiz's newspaper. After that he had had his talk on the phone with Diana. And the Madrid girl on the creaking daybed. He was counting the days until his charter flight home and at times he thought they'd pass fastest if he spent them just sitting on benches in Nice airport.

He drove down into the plain, located the steep avenue after some circling within a one-way system, came up the hill, and saw it was not the same town. The white building was no police barracks but a movie house. A glass case outside showed photographs of scenes from the program; he recognized the American actors but not the Spanish title they had given the film.

Next to the cinema was a restaurant.

A counter with stools, American style. He caught a glimpse of himself in the mirror, unshaven, red-eyed. "Mucho café," he said to the counterman.

"A fellow American," a rotund middle-aged customer in a white polo shirt, sitting at the end of the counter, said. "I spotted you right off, the way you said, 'Mucho café.'"

"What's wrong with it?"

"I'm not sure but it doesn't sound Spanish."

Balthasar shrugged, looked at the menu, and asked for an omelet.

"You don't look like a tourist," the fat man went on. "Not like a commercial traveler either."

"You're a student of your fellow men."

Balthasar's unfriendly voice didn't put the man off. "There's not much else to do here," he answered. "Anything you need to know about this part of the country, I'm the person to ask, I'm a student of everything here."

"You live in this town?"

23

"I'm posted here, we have an air base nearby. I'm Captain Rivers," and he held out his hand. "Recreational services officer."

"My name is Balthasar."

"Balthasar—?"

"Balthasar is my last name. John Balthasar."

"An unusual name," the captain remarked, but Balthasar was saved from having to answer by the arrival of his omelet.

"Names, genealogy, all of that stuff interests me," the captain informed him. "You could say it's my second profession. Here, let me show you something. That omelet's on me if you guess what it is."

He went over to a plaid jacket hanging on the wall behind him and came back with a colored drawing of a shield, on it two wavy blue lines crossing each other, a black ball floating between them.

"It's your coat of arms."

The captain beamed. "Right! You got it right away, eh? *Rivers*. They made that for me in England."

"What does the black ball stand for?"

"That's a cannonball, it symbolizes the military profession."

VIII

Of course Balthasar could have escaped from the captain, but he began to find the conversation soothing, with no need for him to say much back. Also, the captain had grabbed his check. "A bet's a bet," he said.

Captain Rivers repeated his offer of information on any local topic.

"I came here because I thought this was a town I knew. But then it wasn't," Balthasar answered.

"This burg is called Castellar di Santiago. What place are you looking for?"

"I don't know the name. All I know, it's a small town and it has a very large police station, white stone, like a Foreign Legion barracks in an old movie, sitting at the top of a steep, tree-lined avenue."

"A steep, tree-lined. . . ." The captain made a face like a contestant on a TV quiz program. "Easy!" he shouted. "That's easy. You're looking for Huelca. Yes sir. Huelca is the place you're looking for."

"And where is that?"

"A hundred kilometers, say sixty miles, to the north. Midway between Castellar and Pamplona."

"Yes—that would fit—How do you know?"

The captain was beaming again. "Easy as pie. A small town with a large police station, that means the head town of a security district. You see, otherwise you'd find just a little one-room police station, like the cops have here in Castellar. Huelca is such a head town, the only possibility between here and Saragossa. Yes, sir."

"You sure know the local set-up."

"Oh, I know Huelca well. It's quite a place, or was, in the days of the late lamented Caudillo. I've liaised there when there were political security problems."

Balthasar decided not to ask what liaising for political security problems meant.

"That was—" the captain went on—"let me see, that was a fellow called Canti. Yes, Comandante Canti, he ran that show. Good, too. A no-nonsense guy. But he won't be there any more, it's a different ballgame now. Wait." He went to get a map out of his car and marked the road. "Here, take it. I've got dozens of them."

John Balthasar drove into Huelca shortly before noon, as shop-keepers started putting up their shutters. Captain Rivers had been right; it was the town. When he got to the police station the gate was still open and they told him the chief was in.

Balthasar apologized for his scruffy appearance. "I've been on the road most of the night."

"It is urgent then, what brings you here?"

"No, not really, inspector. It's that my vacation time is running out."

"What may I do for you?"

"Do you remember me? Do you recognize me?"

The policeman shrugged. "But of course. It is our profession." He contemplated Balthasar, swiveled his chair around and looked at his bullfight poster, and then turned once more to the room.

25

Balthasar had stood up and went over to the wall near the door. "You have a Wanted notice here which has preoccupied me. . . ." He searched for it with his eyes while he spoke. "I'd like to ask you what you know of the man in question."

The policeman came over to stand beside him.

"Here, him." Balthasar pointed. It was doubtless the same notice, yellowing, with traces of damp on it. But now, studied more carefully, the man in the photograph did not seem to look that much like his 1973 passenger. Perhaps he simply had the same heavy mustache. But I'm never good at recognizing people, Balthasar told himself.

The policeman was looking at him. "But—?" he asked.

"But—now I don't think it's the same man after all."

"Well, let us see. 'Gabriel Amparo, *alias* Sergio—wanted for' how do you say it, 'counterfeit—' an unusual crime in our country —'traveler's checks—' This man cheated you?"

"No, it's not him."

"You must not be afraid of filing charges, Mr—eh?"

"Balthasar, John Balthasar. I'm not afraid, it isn't him."

"This is dated 31 January 1973," the policeman said. "Does that help?"

"Yes, that's to say, no. The man I was thinking of, the man I met, that happened just a year or two ago."

"I do not remember this case," the policeman said. "These papers hang here forever, I'm afraid. We do not keep up." He pulled the notice down, crumpled it up into a ball and tossed it in the direction of his wastepaper basket. He got back behind his desk, and produced a bottle of rum and two little glasses.

"Oh, no, thank you," Balthasar said. "It's too early for me."

"But no. It settles the stomach. So you are looking for a wanted man, Mr Balthasar?"

"Yes, that's to say, the man I was thinking of was not a criminal. This was during the Franco years, it was a political case."

"But you just said it happened a year or two ago. The Caudillo has been dead for eight years."

Balthasar tried a smile. "Eh, well, I guess I'm not quite with it, a night without sleep, you know . . . Sorry to have bothered you, inspector." He picked up the glass which the policeman had poured, took a sip, nodded at him with another smile, and hastened out of there. He half expected a shouted command, one of those Guardias Civil stopping him. There was no one in sight, however, and the gate was still open.

He coasted down the hill and when he stopped at a light, he found himself next to a taxi. "A hotel, where's a hotel?" he shouted at the driver. He suddenly felt hardly able to keep his eyes open.

The cab driver pointed around the corner; when Balthasar followed his direction he came to the entrance of the same hotel as the previous time. There probably wasn't another one in the place, he thought.

The same woman as before was at the reception desk but appeared to have forgotten their quarrel. "Good afternoon, sir. Your room is free."

"Can someone park my car for me? Last time—"

"Absolutamente. I will see to it."

A few minutes later, in the darkened room, Balthasar was asleep.

IX

A booming voice outside his window. He lay motionless, listening; he could not make out a word. He had slept so heavily, he had lost his sense of time.

He got up and opened the shutters. The cobbled square lay in a curious half-light. Many people were standing about. Guardias Civil, some holding torches, were lining a kind of stage from which a priest was speaking. It was his voice which had woken him up. He realized now the priest was speaking Latin, not Spanish. He heard him say "Deo" and "Diabolum". The man was wearing a dazzling, wide-sleeved garment marked with two stripes; he had to be a prelate, someone high up in the hierarchy. Balthasar assumed that an open-air mass or maybe a historical ceremony was in progress but he felt no curiosity about it, only annoyance that they had wakened him. Next to the stage he saw a small group of men and women, completely surrounded by the Guardia Civil, all dressed the same, in a yellow type of robe with red decorations, blades of grass, or maybe flames.

27

Then some of the public turned their eyes toward him and he quickly pulled the shutters back. Huelca wouldn't like a man standing around naked listening to their mass.

He went back to bed but the voice did not let him get back to sleep; it rose and fell and, behind its curtain of words which he did not understand, it seemed to plead and threaten, pull and push at him. Then silence fell. He heard the sound of feet as of people leaving; the pageant must be over. He slept.

Later there was a smell and a taste of smoke. He wearily got up again and pushed at the shutters.

Two wooden poles had been erected in the square not far from his window and a man and a woman were tied to them. At their feet kindling and long logs of wood were piled up.

Several Guardias Civil were holding smoking torches; two priests, one facing the woman, one the man, were reading aloud from missals. Only a few onlookers were still in the square.

The woman was the one nearest to the wall and his window. As Balthasar stood staring at her in terror, a Guardia Civil with a torch approached her.

The priest hastily stepped back.

The Guardia Civil held the flame in front of her face and in that instant Balthasar saw or thought he saw that she was the very same woman to whom he had made love in Madrid. For twenty-three dollars.

The Guardia Civil spoke to her, he smiled. The woman spat at him, then he dropped the torch into the kindling, flames shot up and she uttered a small cry. Balthasar saw her dress, the yellow and red dress he had stared at once in Madrid, saw the flesh of her naked thighs for one second as the dress shriveled up, and then that flesh turning black in the flames.

He turned away; he collapsed on to the bed.

When he opened his eyes, it was morning. His head ached and he felt sick. What a cruel nightmare, he thought.

Then a cold fear took hold of him and his hands trembled as he pushed the shutters far out once more. But the square lay empty; two children were tossing a ball to each other at the far end. No stakes, no stage, no ashes, nothing.

X

His charter flight was to leave from the Nice-Côte d'Azur airport at nine in the evening, which left him with a day in Nice to get through. To save money he had already turned in his car. Fall was in the air. He walked along the edge of the water, the almost imperceptible surf of that sea brushing the pebbles back and forth, the mattresses and deck chairs on the beach empty. The sky was evenly gray with a curtain of rain along half the horizon.

He bought a sandwich at one of the little food stands and sat with it on a seawall.

The turmoil of his Spanish journey had receded, leaving only a vague apprehension. Apprehension of what? He wasn't sure.

It was a Saturday and under the dark sky the lights went on early and the café terraces filled with couples carrying their Saturday shopping. It looked festive to him; it was as if with the approach of autumn, the tourists on their way out, the town became its real self again and showed it with a kind of keen freshness. He was sorry now about leaving and about not having profited more from this long awaited vacation. He had spent all his money on it.

But there was no sense in hanging about. He was early for the airport bus and much too early at the airport. He paced back and forth between the TV-screens with the flight announcements and kept going into restrooms to look at his already fading tan. He was disgusted with himself when he realized he was afraid of the flight ahead of him.

On the plane his neighbors were a Japanese couple who ignored him, talking to each other in high-pitched whispers. In the air, he pressed his face against the window. Blackness, no light anywhere except the yellow light of cities far underneath him. After that, nothing.

When they landed at Kennedy after midnight, New York time, it was still warmer there at that hour than it had been in France. It felt odd to be back so quickly, to stand on a sidewalk suddenly next to a man selling the *Daily News*. He had thought, she knows the flight, we booked it together, Diana might be here to pick me up. But she wasn't.

29

The mail of those weeks was spread out on and beyond the doormat of his apartment and it was all bills and advertisements. The icebox still held an almost empty bottle of vodka and nothing else. There hadn't been very much time, it seemed to him, between his preparations for their journey and his return. He finished the vodka and crept into bed.

At six in the morning, the sun shining from a clean, blue sky, he decided he might as well phone her right then; being awakened would not change her being nice or not-nice to him. There was no answer. He went back to bed and lay contemplating the endless Labor Day weekend, hardly begun.

A Sunday of rattling around in his apartment. He found some Melba toast in a cupboard, he looked at his body in all the mirrors, and went into the hallway to read the headlines of the paper lying in front of his neighbor's door. He turned the TV on and off, picked up the telephone and put it down. It was a great relief when at last the sun dipped behind the houses and it seemed to get a bit cooler. He shaved and left the house.

West 104th Street lay empty. Not a soul. There was a sharp smell in the air which he associated with the bedroom of a girl he once knew—who was she, what was it? Nailpolish remover. Dimethyl ketone. Used to make explosives. A highschool teacher who—He started walking toward Broadway.

As he turned the corner, a cloud of exhaust suddenly enveloped him; a man working on his car was racing the engine. "Fuck you," Balthasar said and saw a pair of threatening eyes on him. He walked on, going uptown.

Here a few people were about. A string of cabs without passengers raced by. The benches in the little parks dividing Broadway were occupied, by black women chatting and watching over their children. They at least looked more or less happy, he thought.

He observed two little boys kicking a can back and forth. One of them missed; his foot slipped over it and he fell. He began to cry and limped to his mother for comfort, and as she hugged him he looked over her shoulder at Balthasar with a kind of triumph on his face.

You have every reason. It's good that you know how lucky you are. Those few years of comforting.

30

He entered the Cuban–Chinese restaurant where he often had his dinner but the man behind the counter was new.

"Nice evening."

"Nice evening." He was the only customer.

Later the place became crowded. He noticed two priests standing about, waiting for a table. He had a slight acquaintance with one of them and he beckoned them over; squeezing his chair close to the wall, he made room at his table. There were introductions; the priest he knew, Father Guillermo Martinez, was also a regular at the restaurant. They talked about the hot weather. Martinez told him he was in charge of a Spanish-speaking parish on the East Side near 110th Street. He was a man with a sharp and sad face, and a short beard which made him look like a soldier in a Velasquez painting.

"My family is from Spain by way of Mexico," Martinez added. "We're not from Puerto Rico."

His companion gave him an amused look.

"I was in Spain this summer," Balthasar said.

"Not a happy country."

"Well, they're doing better now."

"How so?" Martinez asked.

"With Franco gone."

Martinez looked at his colleague who produced a short laugh.

"What's funny about that?"

"An unhappy country," Martinez reiterated.

"Una tierra desgraciada," his friend said slowly, rolling the r's.

That night the two priests appeared in his dream. Precisely as during the evening they came into the restaurant and he invited them to his table. But now he heard himself say, "I was in Spain this summer and witnessed an auto-da-fé. A woman was burned, they had a woman."

"Oh?" Martinez asked. "Where?"

Balthasar was appalled at their calm. "Where? In a place called Huelca. Aren't you surprised?"

The priests shrugged.

"Admittedly, not a pleasant way to die," Martinez remarked.

"You don't say."

"Still, remember, a slow death gives men time to repent and to save their souls," the other priest said.

"But it's sickening, barbaric," Balthasar stammered.

"And, my friend, remember that as a rule at an auto-da-fé they omitted the bellows."

"The bellows?" Balthasar asked but then he woke himself up before the priest could explain those words.

XI

The comfort of taking his regular Broadway bus downtown again to start an ordinary working day.

Labor Day, Monday, he had stayed in, fixed himself the TV dinner he had bought the night before on his way home, and read two whodunits, every now and again glancing at the telephone, which remained silent. But he did not brood any more about Diana; she'd call or she wouldn't. Who cares.

He held a job then at the 42nd Street Library, in the Rare Book division. His journalism period had ended several years before.

It had happened one day when he ran into a man he knew from his Boston college days and was asked what he was up to. He had started describing his current assignment: a piece for a Sunday magazine about which tables in which New York restaurants bestowed maximum prestige on the folks seated at them. "It's all very crummy," he had said, "I'm well aware of it. And it's supposed—" He had stopped himself. They had been standing on the corner of Fifth Avenue and 45th Street, a cold wind was blowing, and he saw that the eyes of the man he was talking to were wandering beyond him.

To his surprise the man had asked, "Well, you want out?" and when Balthasar answered, "Oh yes," he had walked him to the library. "I was once curator of the Berg Collection," he had told Balthasar. He had taken him upstairs and recommended him for an opening he knew of. Balthasar had worked in the college library in Boston, he had done Latin in high school, he had heard of the Codex Aureus. It was enough. It had been settled on the spot and he had happily torn up his first draft on the hierarchy of restaurant tables. The job was low level and badly paid but he rather liked it.

As always it felt good entering the building from the crowded streets. To pick your way through the people waiting for buses, past young men who even at that early hour were buying and selling drugs on the steps, and ending up surrounded by bookcases in a large and silent room. Like a medieval scribe in his cloistered study, while outside people were slitting each other's throats.

He said hello to Susan, the girl who worked in the same room with him at the other end. He asked her how August had been, and she said that he had a nice tan, and that was that. She was friendly but spoke little. She worked unremittingly. Whenever he saw her in a coffeeshop at midday she had a library document propped up in front of her. Balthasar suddenly thought that she was bound to be promoted one of these days. Given the perpetual budget trouble of the library, they might then very well fire him.

He decided not to worry about this.

At lunchtime the day had become very hot. He walked slowly up Fifth Avenue, crossing over to stay in the prism of shade. He felt at peace, not with the world, only with himself, within his own surroundings.

Ignore the rest. Forget that whole sick Spain business, the nightmare. Don't buy a newspaper. That's how people used to live, for centuries. We aren't meant to have no boundary.

When he got back to his desk, he found a note from Susan, who was out: "Diana called." See, he thought, it pays to keep cool. He nodded at the walls of books protecting him.

He waited until five before he called her back. Diana immediately volunteered that she'd been with her mother the Labor Day weekend, and had not phoned him because she had needed to sort herself out. Hubert (her husband) had left for Seattle.

"Oh."

After a silence she said, "You're still mad I flew back when I did."

If she had not left, he wouldn't have gone to Spain. He had not considered that before, and the idea rattled him.

"And did you?" he asked.

"Did I what?"

33

"Sort yourself out."

"Yes."

She suggested they meet for dinner at the Cuban–Chinese place on Broadway. That was code on her part that everything would be all right between them, for she hated the trip back to her apartment in the Village at night. It meant that she'd come with him to his apartment afterward and stay.

XII

Balthasar thought of Diana as clever or with-it rather than intelligent but he was probably wrong about that (his definition of intelligence was academic, dated, male). She looked better in photographs than in life but she was a pretty woman, quite solidly and sensually built, a contrast to Balthasar who was skinny. She was an assistant at *Vogue*, an enterprise she had mixed feelings about, though she disliked Balthasar's jokes on the subject. She had kept her own name through her marriage: Heffernan, Irish, which she often had to spell for people who assumed it was Hefferman and German. During the first World War, her grandfather had temporarily changed his name to O'Heffernan to get away from that.

Balthasar had met her at the film screenings to which he continued getting invited after he was no longer a journalist (someone must have forgotten to take his name off their list). They both always arrived early and used to talk. Only when he came upon her picture in one of those *New York Times* Weekend Section articles, about *successful* young women, did he focus on her face. The idea of going to bed with the owner of that face in the picture filled him with an excitement he had not felt from the nearness of her body.

The next time they met, he suggested a drink afterward, and they ended their evening in bed together. They made love well. As he looked hunched and somewhat sloppy when dressed, she hadn't thought his body would be that straight and hard, and he had not expected her to have such beautiful and firm breasts. And since he considered her a bit silly, he did not act as shy and uncertain as he usually did first time around with a woman.

Because of the elimination of the bottlenecks which once slowed

34

down intimacy, love in an old-fashioned sense may have become almost impossible. With immediate love making it is hard to build up the sense of mystery, to store the energy, needed for such awe. Still, with these two, their bodies suited each other; it became a nice, low-keyed affair. He began to tell himself that here was a girl more glamorous than he could ever have hoped for, and it prompted him to tell her he was in love with her. He thought that otherwise the whole thing would be over very soon.

As for Diana, she was a serious woman but not as serious as she gave herself credit for. The contempt she nursed for her magazine stemmed from her need to feel unthreatened there, not because she objected to its pretence. Her French vacation with Balthasar had been followed by a week of wrangling with her husband at her mother's house; it hadn't been clear why he had been so adamant about Diana showing up there. Presumably he had wanted to spoil her Riviera vacation, which he must have imagined as more sensual and luxurious than it had been. It had ended with the husband leaving once more, for a job in Seattle this time, and Diana deciding that part of her life was behind her for good.

She'd stick with Balthasar.

When she entered the Broadway restaurant, when he saw her walk in followed by the eyes of most of the customers, he was amazed at his own casualness of the past weeks. How could he have been so unpossessive, indifferent even? She was the best thing he had to show for all his years on earth; my best bet, he said to himself. This, this complete person, an entire separate world: think of all the money, all the work spent to get her as she is now, all those schools, hairdressers, tennis coaches, furriers, God knows who, a gallery of men and women to produce this woman who's willing to let me use her body, touch her—.

She sat down. "Don't stare at me like that," she said. "I don't think you recognize me."

"No. Yes. Maybe I never looked at you properly."

"And what do you see?"

"A very beautiful girl. Too beautiful for me."

"Then you're no longer angry?"

"No, no, of course not."

35

"I can tell you, if it helps, I had a horrible time with Hubert." And when he did not answer, "Did you have a good time at all after I'd gone?"

"Well, mixed," he answered. He should not talk about Spain.

She realized he was keeping something from her, and shrugged. "I was properly punished. I had to pay three hundred dollars extra to get on the earlier plane."

XIII

Balthasar Bekker, a seventeenth-century Dutch parson, wrote a book he called *The World Bewitched*, in which he inveighed against the burning of heretics and witches. In fact, he dared suggest there were no witches and there was no devil. These wild ideas were published in Amsterdam in 1691 and made Bekker famous; they also promptly lost him his church.

A descendant of the parson, Jan Balthasar Bekker, he too a religious rebel, emigrated from Holland to the United States in a group of Protestant dissidents led by a Reverend Scholte. In 1847 these people founded the town of Pella in Iowa.

To this Bekker the bitter church arguments about the true nature of the Trinity lost their acuteness in the limitless landscape of Iowa. The complacent egocentricity of the church elders seemed to evaporate between those flat fields and that vast sky, harsh blue in summer, gray so many days the rest of the year.

One early Sunday morning, when Bekker had wandered far from town, he came upon a strange wagon train. Mules and oxen were pulling decrepit broken-down wagons, followed by men, women and children on foot. Women were carrying small children who were clearly dead. It was a silent caravan and when they passed him, they all looked away. These people, he learned later that day, made up the remnants of the Sauk and Fox Indian tribes, expelled from their land. Bekker did not attend Reverend Scholte's Sunday vespers. On Wednesday of that week he left the church and Pella to go east. He dropped the "Bekker" from his name and called himself Jan Balthasar. He was John Balthasar's great-grandfather.

John Balthasar owned a diary of his. It was incomplete and hard to decipher with its cramped handwriting full of Dutch words, but he understood that his great-grandfather had changed his name in protest, detaching himself from the past in a way or proclaiming himself a new man, and he had liked him for it. Beyond that, he had never felt much interest in his family history.

Now he started thinking about the book written by that ancestor of his. The world bewitched.

Perhaps it had a special meaning for him; perhaps old Bekker would like him to take that family name back. The seventeenth century, the century of Descartes, of clear logic, when people thought purely but not without humility, ideas to blow away the sickening chimeras of the present.

You exaggerate again, he said to himself, but couldn't stop believing that book might help him.

The library catalogue listed an English-language copy of *The World Bewitched* and he filed an application for it, but the slip came back marked, "Missing from shelf". Oh well. See.

That evening after work he took the subway to 110th Street and located the church of Father Guillermo Martinez.

The priest opened the door to the rectory himself. He did not look surprised to see Balthasar, but he did not seem pleased either. They sat down in a dark front room looking out on a street noisy with double-parked cars and Balthasar said, "I'm sorry to show up here like this, without calling, but. . . ."

"I'm always ready for someone in distress," Martinez answered.

The word startled Balthasar. "Distress? Well no—You see, I had been waiting for a book and when it did not come—Anyway, there are some questions I just have to ask. About auto-da-fés. Or is it autos-da-fé?"

Martinez stared at him. "Autos-da-fé, I presume. It's Portuguese, you know. In Spanish it would be *de*, not *da*."

"Oh yes?"

"Auto-da-fé, an act of faith. Or perhaps better, an act of The Faith. With a capital F."

"The one and only."

"Yes," Martinez said.

37

"The Portuguese must have invented it then."

"I really wouldn't know."

"I was waiting for a book this afternoon that might have helped me," Balthasar said. "You know I work at the public library, don't you? Anyway. I then started to read about this in the encyclopedias we've got. I know now that the heretics were brought out in yellow robes with flames painted on them, those going to the stake—And the bellows for the unconfessed, the executioner had a pair of bellows with long handles and he blew the smoke away from their faces, to make sure they stayed conscious as long as possible, did you know all that?"

Martinez had several times tried to interrupt and now he held up his hand in protest. "Why are you occupying yourself with this morbid subject?" he asked in a hostile voice.

Balthasar was about to answer, "And here I have told you how I witnessed one", but checked himself in time. That was in a dream. And then in another dream. He shook his head. "It's, it's part of church history, isn't it?"

"And why do you come to me with this?"

Balthasar smiled. "You see, I had a dream in which you yourself were about to explain to me the use of the bellows at an execution."

"A dream?" The priest did not smile back. "I had never heard of all this, all these details. May I confess, I am not attracted by theology and even less by its history. I see the Church as a moral agent."

"Well, tell me then, has your Church ever retroactively expressed its remorse over those deaths by fire?"

"Actually—But you tell me first, are you attracted to the Catholic faith?"

"What does that have to do with it?"

"If you are," the priest said, "you and I may have many talks. If you are not, I see no point in pursuing these obscure historical details with an outsider."

"Have you ever been in Spain, Father?" Balthasar asked in a different voice.

"You asked me that the other day in our restaurant. I had a year's scholarship there, in Salamanca."

38

"Of course. You don't know if Spain had some particularly famous, historic bullfight on the 22nd of June of the year 1941, do you?"

"What odd questions you have, John. I have never been interested in bullfights."

"You see, there's this weird poster. And I met a weird policeman."

The priest waited for him to go on and when he did not, he said, "Spain must have many weird policemen. The 22nd of June 1941 was a Sunday, that I remember. It was the day of the German invasion of Russia. But you must know that too."

"No, I didn't. Or if I did, I'd forgotten. Well, I'm sorry. You must think I'm pretty weird myself." He stood up.

"No, no," the priest assured him. He stood up, too. "By all means, come back if you think there's anything I can really help with."

XIV

And then two days later *The World Bewitched* was brought to Balthasar by one of the stack clerks.

"Thank you, thank you! That was very nice of you, to bother!"

"The library takes care of its own. It must be really important, man."

"It is."

A fragile old book. He held it with pleasure, with relief even, and propped it up against his telephone where he could see it while he finished the morning's cataloguing.

Then it was midday. He opened it carefully and began to read. It was hard going. a rough printing job, and those old f's and s's hard to tell apart without his magnifying glass. He was reading at random.

Here was how God had told the serpent, "Upon thy belly shalt thou go," and whether that meant the serpent had legs before the Fall, that in the Beginning it had been created with legs? Or did it mean only that it had to crawl in sorrow now even as Adam? And why had the Devil not spoken through the parrot, a creature with a

39

voice, rather than through the snake which has no vocal cords?

What is this? Is this the liberating Cartesian logic I was waiting for? But let us go on.

The argument, sprinkled with Latin and Hebrew quotes from the Scriptures, appeared to lead to a questioning of the reality of the Devil himself. But how obscure it all was. . . . poor old Bekker, to be defrocked for this kind of stuff.

Balthasar closed the book. A sense of bewilderment came over him. What did I want with this? What is the matter with me that I suddenly set my sights and hopes on one thing, and then on another, for no good reason? What kind of salvation am I looking for? Let's get this book out of here.

He set out for the stacks behind the Reference Room; it seemed important to get rid of the book and forget about it. Still, he thought, there must be plenty of places today where you can get a heated argument about the serpent and its lack of vocal cords, including presumably the Oval Office of the White House. Maybe I see it all wrong, maybe this was the true courage, old Bekker fighting that cruel and superstitious society of orthodoxy and the stake and the wheel from within, while he was still mired in it himself. Bekker's colleagues turning on him with a hatred of a different order from the vague contempt they must have felt for Descartes or Spinoza, men outside their ken, and Bekker ruined by nothing more than his question marks.

A lesson in this after all. If I understood. My great-and-so-on grandfather. He must have known what would happen to him.

When he went behind the stacks, he found the boy who had brought him the book having his coffee break, sitting on a book box with a container of coffee and reading a newspaper. Balthasar froze to the spot, blinked. The paper the boy was reading was the *Diario de Navarra*. He took the front page by a corner and turned it, to make certain.

The boy looked up only now. "What's up, doc?" he asked.

"Nothing—coincidences."

"You want some coffee?"

"Okay."

Balthasar sat down on another book box. "I brought you that

book back. I thought I'd better take it to you since I didn't sign a slip for it."

The boy got to his feet, folded the paper and put it down. "I'll get you a coffee, doc. You look a bit green in the face."

When he had gone, Balthasar slowly picked up the paper and unfolded it. He saw that its name was *Diario de Nueva York*. But a moment before those same heavy black letters had spelled *Navarra*. He was absolutely certain of that. It was an omen, a portent. A warning perhaps.

XV

A Saturday visit with Diana to her mother, who lived on Long Island near the Sound, in Northport. This was an unprecedented event in their affair.

"She may not like me at all," Balthasar suggested.

"No, she may not."

They went mid-morning in Diana's car. The weather had turned; an evenly white sky sat low over the city and the light was harsh. As they drove through Queens he thought that the city looked its ugliest.

The plateglass store windows were pasted over with discount announcements. Big, dented cars rocked alongside them over the uneven street. At the lights pedestrians stood staring past each other at the Don't Walk signs. "There's sure a lot of broadloom and videos for sale in this place," Balthasar said. "What's broadloom, anyway?"

"You should have taken the parkway."

Then, before Little Neck, came the sudden change to fastidiously green roads. "Here the folks think all's well with the world," he said.

"All is well for them."

"Well, they still have to drive through that mess back there twice a day." After a silence he added as an afterthought, "But I don't suppose it bothers them."

"My mother is bothered."

"And?"

"Oh, she does things."

He made a face. Calf's foot jelly for the poor.

"Don't look that way, please, John. She's a professional, she's not a nice old lady. She works hard. Not just now, also when father was alive. She's on important committees."

Committees? Balthasar thought. For God's sake.

The visit turned out a success, though. On the way back Diana glanced at him—she was driving now—and asked, "Guess what?"

"What?"

"She liked you. She said you were serious, she likes that."

"You sound surprised."

She laughed and gave him an appraising look. "I was. I am."

"Your mother is a discerning woman." He could see Diana was turning it over in her mind, wondering perhaps if there was more to him than she had suspected?

"She told me I could do a lot worse. And then she added, that was typical mother, that in fact I had done a lot worse, hadn't I."

"She didn't like Hubert?"

"No. Poor fellow."

"Why poor?"

"She means to get me an annulment. She doesn't approve of divorce of course. That's a cruel word no, annulment? It will be as if he'd never existed in my life."

"How can she manage that? That's only when a marriage isn't consummated."

"No, it's more subtle than that. There are ways, she says."

"I always figured you had to be inspected by the council of cardinals, to make sure you were still a virgin."

"Please don't be funny about the Church, John."

A silence.

"It is funny, though," he said. "When you think of it, here are the people who've brought us, let's say a hundred thousand deaths by fire, say a hundred thousand men and women who—"

"No, help me, are you on to that again?"

"—who in their day—what am I saying, a lot of them are ready to have another go, hydrogen bombs are the same principle, aren't they and who at the same time—"

"Who at the same time what?"

"Oh, never mind. I'm sorry."

Who at the same time have a God worrying about the sex lives of assistant magazine editors.

He could see that she was quite angry. And pretty, he thought, in her white suit. "Jones of New York," she had told him that morning, "You better like it, it cost a fortune." She had looked so pleased.

He put his hand on her arm. "I am sorry," he repeated.

XVI

As they emerged from the Midtown Tunnel back into Manhattan, a hard, driving rain hit them. It darkened so quickly that the street-lamps lit themselves. She raced up Third Avenue and in the headlights the rain came almost horizontally toward them in cones of bright drops, trucks passing in geysers of water, people huddled under awnings and doorways.

"I like this," she said. "It makes you feel so clean." She made a sudden turn left toward Lexington. "I'm not going to drop you off at your place, I changed my mind, all right? I'm going to take you back to the Village with me."

He parked her car for her and got himself very wet. She had him put on a bathrobe of hers and when she saw he was shivering she lit the oven in her kitchen and left its door open. "Sit next to it," she said. "You have a choice of dinners, all frozen, but not bad."

He had not been in her apartment since before the beginning of the summer. She had never liked him to be there. First she used to say that her husband might be spying on her, but later she announced it simply made her too nervous, it wasn't really right.

"Then why is it right on West 104th Street?"

"North of 96th Street doesn't count with God."

Her kitchen cupboard and icebox were full of samples of new products. "That's from working on a magazine like mine," she told him. "They send us all that modern living stuff."

43

"Shouldn't you send it back?"

"Too much trouble. I'm not being corrupted, I'm not about to suggest to my boss we do an article on the merits of—" she read a label—"Chateau Pom Pom."

They stood at her window and looked down on the rainswept street. A line of honking cars formed, then the road was empty. The traffic lights continued their silent changes from red to green to red to green like signals into space from a dead world. He sighed, and she put her arms around him. "Let's go to bed," she said. "Take off that bathrobe. I'm keeping my clothes on, all right?" She smiled at him and blushed. "Except for my pantyhose."

"You'll—" He was about to say, "You'll wrinkle your Jones suit" but changed his mind in time. She wouldn't have laughed.

In the night he lay awake, staring at the ceiling, on which every now and again a passing car created a pattern of moving lights, incomprehensible parallel lines and triangles slowly creeping from one corner of the ceiling to the opposite one. She had not closed the curtains. She was sleeping, her back against him.

He could feel the coolness of her skin under the warm cover, the cool pressure of her body along its whole length. I'll call this my night with the lights on the ceiling. She breathes inaudibly. Like a cat.

How she had been lying there, her skirt pulled up, her neat blouse, and me naked. Heaven knows what she thought, what fantasy it was. I could see her watch my entering her. A woman's body is my salvation.

XVII

John Balthasar was thirty-six then. His parents had been divorced when he was eight. He had started out at Boston University but left after only one year when his mother died. He had never regretted his leaving; whatever knowledge he had that mattered to him came from books he had read. He had been with Diana for about a year.

Early in 1982, just turned thirty-five, he had sunk into a state of depression, a hopelessness he could not shake off. He managed to do his work at the library, but when he had to pick up an old book or

44

manuscript, its touch, the long weary passage of time he felt in it, frightened him. After work he went straight home and sat staring into space until it was dark and he could go to bed. A doctor he saw prescribed Valium.

One snowy winter morning he had got up early and decided to walk to work. When he turned the corner of Central Park West, he stood still in the thin snow covering the sidewalk. Looking south, he saw a trackless plain, snow glittering in the rising sun as far as the horizon. It was not that he was dizzy, the snow did not blind him. The city had been flattened.

Yet he still knew this was not true. He walked on, his heart beating very fast. Then he saw the little pond in the park shining in the sunlight, the bare trees, and the houses.

He thought, what happened is that I've seen how time may come to a stop. Now, after a billion years, just in my span on earth, a stop may come to human time. But there is nothing wrong with *me*; I am not suffering from depressions but from a premonition. And how could these fail to come? Shocks, a rumbling, a faraway flash of light. That is it, the beginning and the end, no, the beginning of the ending. The blinded people of this city pushing and shoving to get away, cars choking the bridges. We will die in a cacophony of klaxons.

We live in extraordinary times. What I don't understand is that we still mostly function as well as we do.

When spring set in seriously, he seemed to be regaining a hold on himself. On warm days he'd go sit on the library steps at lunchtime and let the voices and music wash over him.

An early English edition of Dante had arrived on his desk. 1802. The first complete translation, the card said. He was to prepare a new catalogue entry and send it on to an outside firm of binders. They were beautiful small books, printed in red and black. He was sorry to lose them so quickly. He phoned the binders and they told him it would be three months.

"Why is that?"

"We can't get to it till June."

"I'll send them over in June then. Just hold my place in the line."

The translator had written a long introduction to the *Divine*

Comedy. That Dante had been in the middle of life when he wrote it, nel mezzo del cammin di nostra vita. Thirty-five years old. And the translator went on, "He had become aware that not by leading the active life, however blamelessly, could he save his soul."

Those words had shocked Balthasar. "Not by leading the active life could he save his soul."

He, John Balthasar, at thirty-five, had not yet lifted a finger to save his soul. He was not sure those words signified a reality, but he was sure that he had done nothing, that he had lived like a cat or a dog, from day to day. He was nothing. If he died, no one would even know he had ever lived.

The certainty of his childhood that he would perform great deeds, or just that his life mattered, had vanished without a trace. He was now halfway down the road of life and he had lost. Was lost.

Susan had that day off; he had moved his desk chair and was reading under a window. At that window in the rays of sunlight falling through the dirty panes, staring at the frontispiece of the first volume which someone had colored in rather crudely, he thought that it mattered not whether you were remembered for a week or for six centuries. The man who had written those books had not been lucky because he was remembered. He had been lucky by living in a time with certainty, when people knew for certain that they had a soul to be saved or to lose.

Think of it, to see yourself in the very center of time and of creation; even with the worst wars and plagues there must have been such a sense of peace and of happiness in that, more happiness than we can ever feel now. In the motionless middle.

And ever since everything has gone by the wayside, first that immobile earth and then the religion of a world four thousand three-hundred odd years old. But then also philosophy and progress and reason and every new hold we found to hang on to, until right now we are down to our minds and souls as organic microchips, programmed to believe in immortality or in liking rock music or the poetry of Dante.

A program just like the one for ants except more complex.

Well, nevertheless. Nothing we can do about it. Grin and bear it. Stop indulging, stop self-pitying. Let that be our saving of souls.

Not long after that day, he and Diana had become lovers.

XVIII

Following his lights-on-the-ceiling night with Diana, he wrote a letter to the Pamplona newspaper *Diario de Navarra*, a letter the stack clerk helped him translate into good Spanish. He was determined now to find Miguel if Miguel was alive, and to find his passenger if his passenger was alive.

An answer came. The *Diario* told him that Miguel Ruiz had retired from the paper in 1979 to write a book. As far as they knew he was living with a daughter in Miami, Florida, for his pension checks went to the Miami National Bank.

Balthasar had a happy day with that letter. He immediately wrote Miguel, care of the bank. How glad to find that you're alive and well, old pal, and in the US, and I hope you remember me, the American journalist at the 1973 trial in Pamplona? And what was the name of the girl Miguel had introduced him to on his last day? And what had become of her and of her boyfriend? And also that he, Balthasar, now worked in the Public Library of New York. What kind of book was Miguel writing? Maybe he could help Miguel with something there.

Miguel's reply was as quick and as intense as if he had waited all those years just to tell John Balthasar about himself.

It was typed, with words run together and myriad errors, a long tale about his miserable pension, the miserable exchange rate for the peseta, the Cuban crooks and *Marielitos* of Miami who pestered him and his daughter and tried to extract money from them for their anti-Castro plans. Miguel's book, the definitive history of Basque literature, was suffering from all this, and yes, he would be grateful for help from Balthasar. The Miami public library had little of use for him and what there was, was usually out or stolen or mutilated, and going to the library and even more going home afterward was taking your life in your hands. He had often wanted to work some weeks in New York. Perhaps after Christmas? Perhaps John could book him in a modest hotel for some weeks?

In his letter, Balthasar had offered his help as a bit of an afterthought, after asking his questions. But these, Miguel had left unanswered.

The letter gave a telephone number and he called. He recognized Miguel's voice but then the man's English seemed to collapse or maybe his hearing was bad now, and his daughter came to the telephone to answer for him.

Balthasar told her that Miguel could stay with him in New York, of course he could, although when he spoke those words he unhappily visualized Diana sitting in his little apartment filled with Miguel's cigar smoke, listening to Miguel's stories, and finally going off home alone. But, Balthasar asked the daughter, what about his query, what about that girl and her boyfriend ten years ago?

He heard a heated discussion at the other end. Come on folks, it's my nickel. "Diez años!" he heard Miguel cry. Finally the daughter came back on with, "Mr Balthasar? Papa wants to come to New York. Next Monday. Shall I call you with the flight number? Can you be called at work?"

Ten o'clock, a cold October evening, Balthasar was at La Guardia, leaning on an Eastern Airlines counter. He saw a very old man approach, a man dressed in a long black overcoat and a cap of imitation fur. He wasn't certain but felt it was safer to smile anyway, and when the man took off his cap, he recognized Miguel. His bald head was covered with brown spots, his shrunken face bristled with white stubble. He had returned to his origins; he looked an old, old peasant.

They embraced.

"You have not changed, my friend."

"Neither have you."

"Yes, yes. I am old. America is not a good place to get old. No friends. But my daughter is a good child."

"Well, there you are, Miguel. Here's one American friend."

"Yes. The flight is early."

"Let's go get your luggage."

"This case is all. We will have dinner. You are my guest. Then you take me to my hotel."

"No, no, you can stay with me."

"Absolutely not," Miguel answered. "Not this time. One day, when you are rich, when you have a wife."

48

Balthasar felt embarrassed; perhaps the daughter had heard the reluctance in his voice, and had told her father? "No, really."

"No, my friend. No argument."

They came out of the East Side terminal into the sharp wind blowing up First Avenue. It made their eyes water and they entered the first restaurant they saw, a place with a German name, dark wood inside, a waiter in a white apron listlessly leading them to a table.

It was oddly like the Pamplona coffeehouse and Balthasar turned to Miguel to comment on that, but Miguel was busy wiping his eyes with a huge handkerchief and then arranging his coat and scarf and hat, which kept gliding down the back of the chair he had hung them over.

XIX

He asked Miguel to think back to that last day in Pamplona, in February 1973, and to the red-haired girl with the fiancé who wanted to get out of Spain.

Miguel did not answer and once more rearranged his imitation fur cap on top of his coat. Balthasar frowned, he tried to hide his annoyance. Why the hell had he got himself into this?

At last Miguel sat down. "I do not answer your question in your letter," he said in an unexpectedly firm voice. "It is not a proper thing to write about."

"Well, be that as it may, I—"

"Tell me, my friend, why did you ask?"

"I have been worried about them, that's all."

"Worried? For ten years?"

Well, fuck him. He was the guy who said, I'm just translating, you don't have to do this. Everyone is a Resistance hero once the war is over.

"I was there, this summer," Balthasar finally answered.

"No shit." The word acquired an exotic character in Miguel's mouth and Balthasar began to laugh.

Now Miguel smiled. "Look, let us not forget we are friends, right? You call, I came." And, looking at his face, "Don't worry, I

49

came not just for you." He patted the case. "My brainchild, my book. In here."

The waiter reappeared to announce that the kitchen was about to close. Balthasar had decided not to reveal that he had already eaten, and Miguel began a spirited effort to order a festive dinner. "You are my guest," he said once more, and asked, what did the waiter recommend? Was the brook trout fresh? But the waiter muttered monosyllabic answers and finally reduced them to ordering the veal scallopini which was featured on signs on all the walls.

"It is not a good question," Miguel finally continued. "In a way, such things were easier to cope with when Franco was alive. Things were clear then, friends on this side, enemies on that side. And now? Now the subject is closed. Now we talk of cars and of apartamientos cooperativos, you understand? Now we pretend that all is forgotten, all is forgiven."

He stopped and seemed lost in thought. The waiter plunked down two sad-looking salads.

"Okay, John," Miguel said. "I think you are the same man you were then. I trusted you then, I trust you now. You want to know about them, I will tell you. The name of the girl is Andrea Amparo."

"Amparo?" Balthasar recognized the name. The Wanted poster.

"Amparo. What is the matter?"

"Gabriel Amparo, alias Sergio . . . He was her husband!"

"No. Her father."

"You're joking."

"Not a funny joke, is it. Her father. Cómo no. Gabriel Amparo. He was arrested in Maya after you had dropped him."

"Oh fuckit, I did not drop him. He walked off."

"Oh."

"He did not give me time to think." The wet snow. Amparo walking back to my car with the little smile on his face.

Another silence from Miguel, another bit of fussing with the fur and the scarf. "Anyway," he then said with a sigh. "Anyway, John. That is all I know of him. We think he may have escaped. No one hears anything afterward. Not a thing."

"He didn't surface after Franco died, after the amnesties?"

"No."

"Why were they after him?"

Miguel shrugged. "I don't remember."

"What? You don't remember?"

"My friend, perhaps I do not want to remember. Perhaps we better not know. You see, perhaps that war is not really over. It may start again one day, no?"

"Now what do you mean by that?" Balthasar muttered.

But Miguel was poking at his meat and asked, "This veal is not very good, is it? I am sorry it is not a better dinner for our reunion. We order coffee now, and brandy."

"I think they want us out of here," Balthasar said.

Miguel looked around. "Yes, you are right." He beckoned the waiter. "No, no, you are my guest. The next time."

They came out on the sidewalk. Miguel shivered, and Balthasar stepped to the curb to get a taxi; they had booked a room for Miguel at the Pickwick Arms.

"How did you know the name Amparo?" Miguel asked when they had gotten into a cab.

"A fluke. A strange coincidence."

"Ah. I don't believe in coincidence. I believe in the logic of history. And how do you get involved in this, I mean, how did you get re-involved?"

"Only in my mind," Balthasar answered.

Curiously, that answer appeared to give Miguel satisfaction. "Only in your mind," he repeated.

"And where is Andrea, the girl?"

"Andrea." He hesitated. "Andrea was arrested later. She was taken to Bilbao. They treat her very, very badly. That is why we think her father had escaped. When she came back to Pamplona, we had trouble recognizing her."

"Oh, Jesus."

"And she was such a pretty girl, no? That lovely hair."

"Where is she?"

"I don't know. She could not get a job. They took away her house."

"Well, didn't you, didn't people, offer to help her?"

"Yes, yes! Of course we did! She did not want our help. She went to Madrid. I fear, I fear very much she became a prostitute there."

51

They had come to the hotel. Miguel Ruiz looked exhausted now, his face was ashen gray. "We will talk more, tomorrow," he said.

"Yes, tomorrow. Good night, Miguel. Sleep well. Welcome to New York."

"Good night, John."

"Miguel, what about the bullfight of June 22, 1941?"

"What, John?"

"It's on a poster, you see it everywhere in Pamplona."

"I never saw that, not when I lived there."

Riding home in a swaying, empty subway car, the idea unavoidably entered John Balthasar's thoughts that his twenty-three dollar Madrid whore had been Andrea Amparo.

Even if it were so, he hastily told himself, it did not matter, what would it matter to her? And if he had smuggled her father across the border in 1973 in the trunk of that damn Opel with the heater that never worked, wouldn't she have been arrested just the same? It was her father who had exposed her to that. He was the man who should have foreseen that danger. He should have taken her with him, of course.

The three of them should have left together that morning and all would have been very different; he would never have let her down, he would have been more afraid of losing her respect than of any Guardia Civil. They'd have driven to Bordeaux, they would have celebrated; he still had his American Express card then.

The maitre d' of the restaurant frowns upon Gabriel Amparo's camouflage jacket and Balthasar takes the man aside and tells him in an undertone that here is a famous Spaniard who just secretly left his country. Wine is brought to their table. The girl keeps looking at him in an intense way, to Balthasar's embarrassment; then the two begin to laugh and she says, "Don't worry, John, this is not my fiancé, this is my father." They all embrace—

Oh cut it out, he thought, it's ten years later. You're a slob.

He became aware of a strange music just audible over the rattling of the train, and then the connecting door opened and a dirty, wildly dressed man entered the car, closed the door behind him, and continued playing an instrument Balthasar had never seen before, a kind of small tuba. He walked through the car playing until he stopped in front of him. He looked threatening, Balthasar thought, and wondered if it was cowardly to give money. The musician muttered "Por favor" and grinned. Balthasar found two quarters in his pocket, the change from Miguel's cab, and handed them over.

The girl in the Madrid bar. Wasn't her hair red but dyed black? Who'd think of dyeing hair of such a lovely color and making it look like everyone else's in Madrid if it wasn't in order not to be recognized? How many young women have their front teeth missing?

If she were Andrea it does matter, because the coincidence would be too much. I don't believe in coincidences, Miguel said. No, he said I don't believe in coincidence, only in the logic of history. But here is no logic. It is impossible she was Andrea.

But the whore who took her dress off for five dollars extra did wear a yellow dress with red flames, the *sanbenito* they put on heretics, the drawing I saw in that nauseating woodcut in the Spanish encyclopedia. And if such a string of coincidences is to be ruled out, then the logical conclusion has to be, I had some girl in Madrid and all the rest, the hair and the dress and the auto-da-fé exist only in my own mind.

He became very frightened now. Insanity means, the murderer and monster are inside you. I'm overwrought, I still have that prescription. I'll get myself some Valium tomorrow. Diana was right when she suggested I go see her analyst, except that she can afford him. What would such a man tell me, that the normal state for people is to be calm and happy?

The Wanted notice was real for that is how I recognized the name when Miguel mentioned it. I did not imagine that. And Miguel and his plastic fur cap exist, they're not imagined.

But then it is real *and* coincidence. How do I know that that notice isn't still hanging in half the police stations of Spain. Maybe I focused on it because I wanted to find that man again, maybe I left that car blocking a little street in the first place because of an unconscious association: man I'm looking for, police, parked car leads to police. That doesn't sound crazy now, does it. What do I know. Some kind of Freudian connection. Or, simpler, a man wanting to save his soul, gets himself to a police station where he will find a clue to his search. A door to the past.

Ninety-six and Broadway. He automatically got up to change for the local train. I do function, he thought.

XX

He was standing with Diana at the reception desk of the Pickwick Arms to pick up Miguel Ruiz. They were going to cook dinner for him at Balthasar's apartment; that was Diana's idea. "Latins like it when you receive them at home instead of taking them to restaurants," she had said. "I'll bring some good stuff from my treasure-trove."

Sometimes her vocabulary made Balthasar wince but he had learned to keep quiet about it.

"Mr Ruiz asks you to come up," the receptionist said. "Room one forty-six."

"No! We're double-parked," Balthasar told him. "Can you get him back on the phone?"

"Never mind, I'll wait in the car," Diana said. "You go get him, it's nicer."

When he came to Miguel's door he heard a buzz of voices, and to his surprise the room was packed; people were sitting on chairs, on the bed, and on pillows on the floor. There were bottles and glasses and the air was thick with tobacco smoke.

Miguel hugged him. "John. A big reunion here. Come meet these nice people."

"But you were going to have dinner with us."

"Of course, of course! But it is early, it is seven. Your fiancée —when does she expect us?"

"She's downstairs in her car, waiting."

"What? This is terrible. Come with me. Excuse us," he called out to his guests who had been looking curiously at Balthasar.

When they stepped out into the street, Miguel spotted the car and opened Diana's door. "I am John's friend from Spain. You must please come upstairs and have a drink with us. Let me have the key, please. We take care of your car."

She gave him the keys with a smile and he took them to the doorman in the lobby.

"That guy doesn't park people's cars," Balthasar muttered, but the doorman and Miguel were laughing and the man accepted the keys and nodded at Diana.

In the elevator Balthasar noticed that Miguel smelled of peppermint and brandy. A good combination. He looked spirited, less fragile. "Miguel, New York agrees with you," he said.

"I see old friends, and beautiful women," Miguel answered and beamed on them both.

Back up in the hotel room, Balthasar was introduced to a man who was some ten years younger than Miguel, very wiry and erect. "This is Julian Lucas," Miguel said. "He and I have not talked for forty-four years, and he recognized my voice when I telephoned him. How about that."

The two slapped each other on the back.

"This fellow was a captain in the Spanish army," Miguel told Balthasar. "He came to this country in 1939 when the Republic had lost the war. In 1941 he joined the American army."

"In the American army I was a corporal," the man said with a laugh. "They did not trust me."

"Julian came specially because he may be able to help you," Miguel went on. "It seems he knows more about our friend."

"Our friend? You mean—"

"Amparo. Of course. Gabriel Amparo."

"We will talk," the captain-corporal said. "You call me. Now you must introduce me to your beautiful wife."

"Girlfriend," Diana said.

"Marry soon," from Miguel.

"Captain?" Balthasar asked when the two of them were standing alone in a corner with glasses of rum, in a sudden silence.

"Corporal, my friend."

"Corporal. Mr Lucas. What became of Gabriel Amparo? Is he alive?"

"You call me, young man. We'll make a date. Miguel will give you my number."

"Okay." He took a sip.

"You don't like rum," Lucas remarked.

"Is he alive or dead?"

Lucas frowned and then answered, "Alive."

55

"How weird that no one—" Balthasar began, but seeing Lucas's unresponsive face, he did not finish his sentence.

Miguel was reluctant to be drawn on the subject of Julian Lucas once they had left the party in the hotel room and were driving uptown through the foggy park. His jolliness about the captain-corporal had evaporated. "He's become a queer fellow," was all he would say.

"Did he tell you what he knows about Amparo?" Balthasar asked.

"I didn't want him to. I told you, John, I live for my book now, I'm a very old man, I can't afford the time. I can't afford the battles."

"Battles? What kind of battles?"

But Miguel wouldn't answer that. He smiled at Diana. "What are you cooking for our dinner, novia of John?" he asked her.

Balthasar did telephone and make an appointment to go see Lucas. Diana, who was right then unusually patient with his notions, wanted to come along, "to inject a note of sanity" as she said, "in all this agonizing."

He had finally told her about the dreams.

Julian Lucas lived in an apartment on the ground floor of a neglected Riverside Drive building, crammed with photographs and odds and ends. "They're trying to get us all out," he told them as they looked around, "but they won't succeed with me. Landlords. No Pasaran." He kept dashing in and out of his small kitchen, bringing olives, other snacks, glasses, ice. He served rum. "Welcome," he said, lifting his glass, then vanished again to get napkins.

"He seems very sweet," Diana said.

On the wall facing them was the Spanish Civil War photograph by Robert Capa, of the Andalusian infantryman shot as he stands up to advance, dropping his rifle, still on his legs but falling backward, in the split second between life and death. It was a very large print, and around it were glued old colored postcards, "Help Defend Madrid", "Smash the invasion of 1936 as we did in 1808", but also a picture of the defenders of the Alcazar fortress being embraced by Franco. A photograph of Lucas as a young man but

56

easily recognizable, looking out from the balcony of a ruined house over a bombed street. "A million dead," Balthasar said to Diana. "Past history."

At last Lucas sat down. "Now," he said. "What are we getting into, and why?"

Balthasar hesitated. Why indeed. What did he know or want to know of the intrigues, the battles as Miguel said, of these people presumably still fighting a war of fifty years ago in their overheated little exile rooms, while in Madrid the conversation was of co-op apartments and the price of gas? But the night before, lying awake in his apartment, listening to a police siren traveling up or down Broadway, it was impossible to tell which, there had been the creaking daybed again, the wet snowflakes. He took a deep breath.

"John—?" Diana said.

"Yes. You told me, Mr Lucas, that this man, Amparo, is alive. If you know that for sure, and if you know where he is, I want to get in touch with him. I have to talk to him. I think Miguel explained to you—"

Lucas shook his head to interrupt. "No, he refused to elaborate. And I'd like to hear it from you directly, anyway."

"Why the mystery, Mr Lucas?" Diana asked.

"Yes, I wonder about that, too," Balthasar said. He pointed at the pictures on the walls. "That is all past history, no? Is Mr Amparo still in hiding? How could he be?"

"No one is in hiding," Lucas answered. "Democracy has triumphed, hasn't it?"

He sounded ironic, but he seemed to be waiting for an answer. "Well, yes," Balthasar said. "Hasn't it?"

"Yes. There's another aspect to all this, privacy. Now, I've been an American citizen for forty years, I'm as good an American as anyone in this room; still, I'm a Spaniard too, my blood is Spanish . . . Privacy isn't always valued here. We Spaniards value it very highly."

"And so?"

Lucas sighed and held out the plate of olives to each of them in turn. "Yes, Amparo is alive," he then said, "and he lives in this country."

57

"No kidding! That is very good news to me. So what's the problem?"

"You want to see him—why? To tell him you're sorry you left him in the lurch?"

Balthasar felt himself redden. He realized Diana was staring at him but he did not look at her. "Yes," he said.

"It's ten years ago, John. I may call you John? The friends of my friends—Do you really think he's still waiting to hear this?"

A silence.

"John here is a strange bird," Diana said. "We don't understand it ourselves but he's had nightmares and stuff about this. Ever since he happened to find himself back in Spain this summer."

"You went back to Spain?" Lucas asked.

Balthasar nodded. "I can quite see that Mr Amparo, wherever he is, whatever has happened to him since, may not. . . ." He let the sentence die out and said, "I'm sure he doesn't give a damn. But I do, for my own peace of mind. I'm guilty of something. If I were a Catholic, I'd go to confession."

"And a letter? A letter in which you explain yourself?"

Balthasar shrugged and did not answer.

"You want a meeting. Very well, a meeting it shall be. You may have to travel some considerable distance. I trust you do not mind. I will see what is to be done. Now please eat and drink. This is smoked squid. Ah, I forgot, you do not like rum. But I—"

"No, no, I assure you, it's fine. I like this."

"See, John," she said afterward, "These obsessions of yours. For nothing. I bet you Amparo—But aren't you relieved?"

"Oh, I am. But isn't that Lucas a strange bird? And first he said he knew nothing, and then he showed he knew all about it."

"Oh, so what. Don't forget, he's very spruce, but he is an old man. They have their ways."

"What were you going to bet, that Amparo *what*?"

"That he's become a rich businessman, or a speculator, something of that sort, that's why he doesn't want any reminders from his past."

"What makes you think that? He sure wasn't that type."

"You don't have to defend the man against me. I have no

objections to rich businessmen. You know, I think you're almost sorry there isn't a big drama for you to go through, some unmarked grave in a Spanish prison yard."

Maybe so, he thought, maybe so. Maybe I needed carrying him around with me. My passenger.

"I'm sorry, John," she said. "Everyone is a psychiatrist right? Anyway, you didn't leave him in any lurch, it was him getting out of the car. Wasn't it? Didn't he? Oh, Mother of God, what are we talking about, it's ten years later."

XXI

He did not hear from Lucas for two weeks. He had a bad time and prescribed himself back on his Valium of the year before. Avoiding his few friends, he turned only to Diana—excessively, he realized. But the unease tugging at him went away when they were alone together. Making love to her put him at peace.

She now mostly stayed overnight at West 104th Street although she hated the place, and if she was aware that she was being used in a way, she didn't let on: the thinking which explains lust as a wish to return to the womb or anyway not as a wish to make love, was not her style. She had often looked on Balthasar as a bit wishy-washy and he bored her when he circled around and around some idea or other. Now all that vanished in the intensity with which he wanted to see her naked, to touch her, to have her.

Lucas telephoned. He announced that he was "delivering the goods": Amparo was ready to meet Balthasar. "That's to say, you have to go see him of course."

"And where is that?"

"That's in or near a little burg called Paolita, and that's in southern Florida."

"Oh—"

"John? Don't tell me you're changing your mind?"

"No, no, I'm not."

"Okay then. Let me give you the scoop. And he's calling himself Captain Willers, don't forget. W-i-l-l-e-r-s. Forget 'Amparo'."

*

59

Balthasar had to travel there during a weekend as he couldn't get time off at the library. He also had to find two hundred and fifty dollars for the plane fare. But he told himself and Diana that he must see this through now, once and for all.

She was all in favor. "You'll save the money in Valium," she said.

The meeting was set for the following Saturday at three.

It was nearly noon when he arrived in Miami. Following Lucas's instructions he took a local bus to Naples, a miserably slow ride. When he got out at Paolita a warm rain had started to fall. He went into the bar across from the bus stop where a fat-bottomed man in work clothes waved him over and asked, "You Balthasar?"

"Yes. You're here for Willers, right?"

"Captain Willers. Right. Let me finish my beer. You have one?"

Balthasar took his raincoat off and sat at the bar. There were many men, no one talked, there was no television. They all seemed to stare at the picture of a naked lady above the bar, who had a clock by way of figleaf.

"In here everyone always knows what time it is," his companion remarked.

"How far is it, to Willers's place?"

"Only a couple of miles."

They set off in a station-wagon at a great clip. Neither of them said anything, there was only the sound of the tires on the road, and the clicking of the nails of a German shepherd dog in the back of the car, keeping its balance in the curves by little steps to and fro on the boxes they were carrying.

The odds are Amparo never for a moment believes I'm here for my own peace of mind, if that's what Lucas told him. What's this Captain Willers bit, anyway? Maybe he thinks I'm still a journalist. Jesus, this is a miserable spot all right.

They were driving down a narrow road in a flat landscape, on each side flooded fields or perhaps swampland, low clouds, a gusty rain, and threads of fog across the road.

"Is this a farm we're going to?" he asked.

"Sure, and a big one too. You'll be surprised."

Fence appeared on the right, and then a high gate. The driver got out and unlocked it. A sign said, "Center for Crop Disease Control. Danger. Absolutely No Trespassing". They stopped in front of a lodge built of logs and stone. And there with the same mustache and in what looked like the same camouflage jacket, was his 1973 passenger Gabriel Amparo clipping a hedge in the rain.

XXII

Balthasar got out after a tangle with the dog which insisted on getting out at the same time. Amparo hugged the dog and let his face be licked before he shook hands with Balthasar.

"So you came all the way from New York. Enter."

They sat down in a neat living room. A boy who had been watching television was sent away. "And tell 'em in the kitchen to bring us some food," Amparo said to him.

The two men looked at each other.

Amparo had changed; there was gray in his hair and he had developed a paunch. More important, that quality of his of being above it all seemed to have vanished, that cool little smile Balthasar remembered so starkly from ten years ago and which had played such a role in making him feel inadequate, "a slob" was the word he used for himself. He thought that Amparo now looked more of a slob than he. He thought that this visit would serve its purpose and that it would lift a weight off his shoulders he might have put there himself.

"So you came all the way from the Big Apple. To get absolution from old Gabriel Amparo."

Balthasar frowned at him.

Amparo smiled. "Don't get heated. I remember our little drive too, like yesterday. I think it's great, you worrying about it so long, and coming to tell me to my face. I told Lucas, I sure appreciate this, I said. No shit. But, you're too late. Gabriel is dead and buried, has been for a long time. Meet Captain William Willers."

Balthasar did not answer. He didn't care what Amparo thought or said about his visit.

"Yes. I think it's great," Amparo repeated. "But you know what, you weren't guilty. Of nothing. No more than I was, anyway, and

61

the rest of that half-assed bunch of sons of bitches. You know what, when all's said and done, you did me one big favor."

"How's that?"

"Never mind, take my word for it."

The boy reappeared and put down a tray with plates of rice and seafood and cans of beer.

"Here, John, take this beer," Amparo said and he started eating, explaining between mouthfuls that the shrimp and the scallops were fresh caught, dropped off by a friend who was a trucker with a run between Miami and Sarasota.

Balthasar opened his beer. "I don't really want to eat now," he said, "I'd rather try and catch the five o'clock plane back. The next one's not until nine tonight."

"You're joking! You mean, this is it? This is what all the commotion was about? Lucas practically crying in the phone about you?"

"Well, you see," Balthasar started uneasily, "it was the idea that I hadn't measured up to some—I don't know. Anyway. Who cares, here you are hale and hearty."

"I know what's eating you," Amparo told him. "Eating—not eating—get it? It's that you had figured me for some kind of hero, a martyr, and here I'm just a happy farmer, right, clipping his hedges on Saturday afternoon. Am I right?"

"No, no, not at all. I'm not hungry, they serve lunch on the plane, and I have to get back."

"Lunch on the plane. That chickenshit wrapped in plastic? Look, Jeff will put you on your plane, I'll have him drive you to Miami, okay? Try these shrimp."

Balthasar took a plate and complied. They ate in silence, Amparo bending his head to his plate and giving Balthasar looks from halfway down. "Just a fat farmer, eh?" he asked.

"Well, you're a kind of botanist, aren't you? It says on the gate that—"

Amparo interrupted him. "I think it's great you worried enough to come all this way! I really do! I appreciate it. I'll show you. I'll show you I still trust you."

"Thanks." Balthasar was embarrassed by the outburst.

"Come with me. I'll show you something that'll surprise you." He got up and struggled back into the camouflage jacket which he had hung on the back of his chair. "You didn't waste your time with a botanist, take my word."

XXIII

They went around the house followed by the dog, crossed a field and entered a small wood. It was dark under the trees. They crossed a creek on a little wooden footbridge.

Amparo looked at his watch. "Time is just right," he muttered. "Pretty wild here, eh? We're next to the National Park. No one ever comes here, not even on the Fourth of July. Of course it's fenced, too."

They heard the sound of a whistle, and Amparo called his dog and put it on a leash. "Just ahead."

At the edge of the treeline he stopped. In front of them lay a landscape of sand and little ponds, interspersed with clumps of bushes and dwarf palm trees. The rain had slowed to a drizzle and all around them was the sound of dripping water. Rows of men in camouflage jackets were plodding through the sand and the water without bothering to go around the ponds. They were some two or three hundred feet away and Balthasar could not distinguish their faces in the misty air; they wore helmets and carried automatic rifles. A man closer by blew that whistle again, and the men dropped down and became almost invisible as they crawled on their bellies through the rain.

"Isn't that something?" Amparo asked beside him. "Isn't that a sight?"

Balthasar thought it was a dismal sight but he only said, "Yeah—"

"I'll just go over," Amparo said. "Just wait here, don't get yourself more wet than you have to." He ran over to the man with the whistle and the two could be seen arguing.

When Amparo joined him again, he was panting. "Let's get back, I'm soaked. You've seen what there is to be seen."

"You're training mercenaries?"

"Volunteers. You didn't expect that when you saw me clipping that hedge, did you? I'm still in there, keeping up the fight."

"Against Franco?"

Amparo looked at him and then burst out laughing. "You're okay, John."

When they came around the house, a red Ford coupe had pulled up next to the station-wagon.

"My girlfriend," Amparo said. "Now, you still feel you wasted your time with me?"

"How do you get away with this?" Balthasar asked.

"Who's to stop me? We're running a self-defense school. Uncle Sam and me are like this." And he crossed his fingers. "Yes, John. I came out on top in the end. I'm on your side now."

Two or three times Balthasar had been on the verge of asking Amparo about his daughter and decided against it. But since the man was so self-satisfied . . . "And what about Andrea?" he asked.

"Andrea? My daughter? What about her? She's fine."

"Miguel said—"

"Miguel said what?"

"Wasn't she arrested at that time, after you'd escaped? He said she was brutalized by the police, her teeth knocked out, I don't know what else, no one would give her a job, the house was taken away, and she just, she just vanished, no one knows where."

"Miguel Ruiz is an old woman. He always was. Andrea is fine."

Balthasar eyed him. If Amparo was lying, it didn't show. "Well, I'm really happy about that. That's worth my trip. You don't know how I brooded about it."

A frown from Amparo. "But what's Andrea to you? You only met her for about one fucking minute, ten years ago."

"Yes, true.—I thought I had seen her again, but I was mistaken."

"Again? And where would that have been?"

"In New York. Where else."

A young woman came out of the house and walked up to them under a red umbrella. "Everything all right?" she asked Amparo.

"Fine. Here, say hello to my friend John. John, this is Rosa."

The woman smiled at Balthasar. "Hi, John. Aren't you coming in?"

Balthasar shook his head. "I shouldn't, I really have to get back to New York."

Amparo held out his hand. "You climb in the wagon and I'll send Jeff out to you. He'll get you to Miami in no time at all. You know, that was great, you coming out all the way here. Wasn't that great, Rosa? You still feel you wasted your day, John?"

"No, of course not. Thanks for the shrimp."

"Remember you got a friend here now, a man who trusts you. Where you live?"

"West 104th Street. Near Broadway."

"We'll be in touch, John. Give my regards to Broadway. And here—" He struggled to get his hand under his jacket and came out with some folding money.

"No, no. Thank you."

"Just to help you with the trip, John. Don't tell me you can't use it."

"No, really not. I'm fine."

"Oh okay then. No offense meant. Say goodbye to my friend, Rosa." He put his arm around the woman's shoulder and led her into the house.

Balthasar got into the station-wagon, relieved that Amparo hadn't tried to make him stay longer, but surprised about that too. Well, fuck it, enough of this scene.

Jeff came out of the house and squeezed himself behind the wheel. He took a pint bottle of rye out of his pocket which he handed to Balthasar. "The boss says, for you to keep warm. Don't worry now, you're going to catch that plane."

XXIV

Back in his apartment, he called Diana and told her about the visit. He didn't mention the men in the flak jackets.

"So the search for Mr Amparo is over and done with," she said. "You're Free At Last."

"That's how it feels, you're not kidding. I've already washed my Valium down the john."

"I'm very glad, I'm very, very pleased."

"Say—why don't you come over and see me."

"It's too late. I'm bushed. Come on down here tomorrow morning, as early as you want. We'll celebrate your deliverance. I'll make you Sunday brunch. Maybe I'll have a surprise for you too."

He didn't really mind being alone; it would be good to test out this feeling of having his passenger off his back, as he called it. He drew a bath and, stretched out in the big, rust-stained tub, he purposely tried to conjure up his old feeling of guilt. It stayed away. So far, so good.

On the plane home he had decided Amparo was lying about his daughter, for why would Miguel make up a story like that? The man had sacrificed his daughter, just as he had sacrificed his Spanish civil war beliefs, hadn't he? "I'm on your side now." Little did he know. Now he was Captain Willers speaking a TV kind of tough talk and owning a police dog and a chauffeur who called him "boss". Running a camp for men trailing Sten guns or whatever they had through the mud, readying themselves for God knows what—but it wasn't even a matter of "politics", of switching from left to right, it was that the 1973 Amparo had emanated some sort of above-it-all integrity, that's what he had, wrapped into that little smile as he walked off in the snow. It put others to shame. Others like me. The 1983 Amparo is just another slob pursuing his own little or big racket and liking his food and drink and enjoying his piece of ass (as he doubtless calls it) named Rosa.

So what difference does it make, if he now deals in real estate or trains mercenaries to knock off the opposition to some little Franco or other. I wasn't his keeper in 1973 and he is no man's and no woman's keeper and no child's keeper in 1983.

But let's by all means keep Miguel out of this. Miguel said that he wants to stay out of it anyway. But if he heard about men in US Army helmets jumping around in Florida at Amparo's whistle, there's no saying what he'd think he had to do about it. How I'll handle this, I'll stay away from Miguel for a couple of days. (Miguel was working in the library Writers' Room, where Balthasar had managed to get him desk space.) And after that I will simply not mention Amparo any more. Miguel will do his work in peace.

Balthasar had a sense of physical well-being. Everything was under control, finally. He lifted a leg out of the water and studied it. He touched himself but stopped. Keep it for Diana tomorrow. He got out of his bath and went to the dark living room with a towel around his middle, and stood at the window.

Suddenly he shivered. Isn't it cheap of me to assume this new Amparo, Captain Willers, let me off the hook? Am I jumping to conclusions too quickly? Who knows what he's been through, what those Guardias Civil in Maya did to him when they'd caught him, who knows what the man lived through in all those years of hiding.

No. Don't let me relativize this now. There must be a continuing reality to a man's life, I don't believe in the old Amparo with the little smile any more. He never existed.

Rectifying the past, reconciling it, is not an illusion. It cannot be.

XXV

When Diana opened her door for him, he was struck by her appearance. She looked different that Sunday morning, less solid. Perhaps it was just that she looked pale. But that touch of everyday good looks she had, something almost plain, a bit common, had vanished. There was a dreamlike quality about her, he thought. No, not dreamlike, that's idiotic; what they used to call spiritual.

She was in a white flannel bathrobe. "A celebration," she said. "But I'm not very energetic today. I'll pour your coffee and that's about it."

He kept glancing at her. I've never seen her like this, he thought, I must have been terribly wrong when I imagined her to be just a bit stupid, a bit corny. She can't be, not with that face. How hard it is to judge a woman.

"So there you are, a new man. Tell me more about that expedition. Say, I figured you'd come back with a new tan."

"It rained. A warm creepy kind of rain. And there's little more to tell. I'd built up some kind of, well, what, in my mind and then . . . Oh, let's forget Lucas and Amparo. I'm going to. They're just creeps, those guys."

"Miguel is a very nice man."

"Of course. I'm not talking about Miguel. Miguel dropped them too. It's history."

When she asked no question, he went on, "I'm taking good care of him, of Miguel. I got him well ensconced. We talk every day, we walk around at lunchtime, eat our hamburgers together. He's crazy about you, you know."

She smiled. "He must have been a terrific swordsman in his day."

"Swordsman? Where do you get that revolting expression? And Miguel is as ugly as sin."

"Maybe. He's got it, though."

"Got what?"

"Oh John. Have some more coffee."

He studied his hand as he reached for the coffee cup. Have I got it? I know what she's talking about all right. Miguel has I don't know what. Weight, for lack of a better word. Me, I'm a slob, great-grandson of a preacher, a Dutch dominie full of question marks. I'll never keep this girl.

"Every day Miguel asks why we don't get married," he told her.

She smiled again.

"*Shall* we? Shall we get married?"

To his astonishment, she blushed.

"Shall we? Diana?"

"Yes, and why not," she answered.

"Are you serious?"

"Well, yes. I'm starting to say 'well' as much as you do."

"Then it's all settled?" he asked.

"All settled."

He gave her a doubtful look. "That easily?"

"You're sorry already. Too late. You can't get out of it any more."

He stood up to kiss her. "Tell me about the surprise you have."

"But you know already, it's that we're getting married."

Diana's Hubert had been married once before, which meant that her marriage to him did not count from the strict Catholic point of view and that the annulment would be that much simpler. Hubert on his side had started divorce proceedings in the state of Oregon where the rules were apparently very liberal. Soon, as she put it, she'd be as good as new.

68

"But I wonder now how I got you," he said to her. "Why didn't you end up with one of those glamorous types who hang around at your magazine?"

"You sound jealous."

"I am."

"Don't be. Those men aren't interested in me. They aren't interested in any woman; they are one hundred percent self-centered. You know, they don't make love to you because they desire you or not even because they need a girl the way a sailor in port does."

"Why do they then?"

She began to laugh. "The theory in my office is, they need someone to admire their erections with them."

"Oh—" He stared at her.

"Do I shock you?"

"Well, yes. No. How do you figure in this, did you, eh, I mean what about those ideas of yours about sinning?"

"I've been to confession. Last Saturday. I'm pure."

"It's sure an easy system," he said.

"No, not so easy."

XXVI

A few days later Diana's mother appeared at the public library just before noon. She'd come to take Balthasar for a drink, she announced. They went to the Hibernia Club. "My husband and I used to meet there after work, once a week. Long ago."

She stared for a long time at the portrait of a nineteenth-century gentleman hanging above the fireplace of glowing imitation logs, and seemed lost in thought. When she turned to Balthasar, she made a visible effort to focus on him and on the present. "That's Robert Emmet," she said, making a move with her head in the direction of the picture. "Probably painted after his death, by someone who never met him."

Balthasar, who didn't know who Robert Emmet was, made a polite sound.

"Yes. Hanged by the English at the age of twenty-five. Would you say this world of ours has made much progress through the years?"

"No."

" 'No' gets my vote too. But to talk about Diana. You may have noted that she has a somewhat, let's say, simplified view of life."

Balthasar hesitated. "If I understand what you mean by that, maybe so. But don't most of us? That's what the media have done to us."

"I'm glad you still think media is plural. Yes, maybe. I blame them a lot. Especially that magazine she works on, I can't stand it, it's so breathless."

He wondered what she was going to tell him or ask him. She looked grim. Nice though. Very well put together still. Comforting, if it was true that girls always ended up looking like their mothers. But by that time he'd be out of it, he'd be about eighty; no need to worry about Diana's looks then.

"Of course all that is on the surface," Mrs Heffernan said. "I'm quite aware of that. The real evil is somewhere else."

"What is your 'real evil', Mrs Heffernan?"

"Ah."

A waiter appeared; Balthasar asked for Scotch and she ordered the same for herself.

"If you and Diana are to be married, to be married in church that is, we have to apply for dispensation. Were you baptized, John?"

"I'm not sure. Does it matter to you?"

"It will matter to you," she answered, "one day."

"What about—" He was going to ask about Hubert but then decided that would be in bad taste.

She had guessed, though. "She married Hubert on the sly, in front of a justice of the peace in Maryland. It didn't count. Now she wants to get married in church."

"In front of God."

"Yes."

"I appreciate the symbolism of being baptized," Balthasar said. "I envy Dante for it. In an Einsteinian universe, if that's a word, it doesn't seem to belong. Or to make sense."

Unexpectedly she smiled. "Don't be a pedantic ass, John."

"Sorry. Never the less—"

70

"To sum it all up," she said, "you're not a Christian, you haven't got a penny to bless yourself with, you live on the same block as a cleaning woman I used to have, you have no family, you're almost forty—"

"Thirty-six."

"—but you never got married, which is almost as bad as that Hubert of hers who had himself married the first time when he was twenty-one."

"Well, actually, Mrs Heffernan, about the respectability of one block in Manhattan over another, that's a joke now, it's a miracle I live anywhere. My family goes back quite famously at least to the year 1691 when a Dutch ancestor of mine exposed some of the more lethal errors of your church one more time, and as for my age, I assure you it doesn't mean I'm a crypto gay if that's what you were worried about."

"You'd say then of yourself that you're a good catch."

"A good catch? That's out of Jane Austen."

"Let's say then, good marriage material."

He thought about that. "No, maybe not."

"And why not?"

"Because I have times of great desperation. I'm not a nice normal guy."

"Diana tells me—"

"Then again, maybe it isn't quite normal any more to be normal."

"Diana tells me you have nightmares, about auto-da-fés."

"I need her, that's for sure. I need her sanity."

Those words made an impression on Mrs Heffernan. She frowned, emptied her glass, studied Balthasar's face. "Our Judaeo–Christian–Humanist country, Mr Balthasar, if that's what we are, is as ready to burn heretics as the Catholic Inquisition ever was. The heretics live farther away, that's the only difference."

He looked at her with great surprise.

"My husband used to say to me, 'Our politicians are ready to declare God's adventure with mankind a Dead End.'" She had a little laugh. "What's the matter, did you think I was an Irish society lady, worried mostly about juvenile delinquency reaching Northport?"

71

"No, no, certainly not."

"You see, I may be more on your side than you knew."

XXVII

They were to be married in a little church, St Joseph's in the Village.
That was a compromise, Diana had wanted something more
fashionable, and perhaps her mother too, although she didn't say.
Balthasar had vaguely held out for a more "ecumenical" setting.
What he meant with that, he couldn't define. You married in church
or you didn't, Diana pointed out to him, and even New York did not
have a church for both Catholics and Protestants. "Ecumenical"
meant depressing halls decorated with arabesques. Then he had
looked forward to a mental battle with the priest who was to marry
them: if a church wedding, it had to have the sharpness of a
confrontation. When it turned out that no one showed any desire to
argue with him, that all they asked was an imprecise statement
about the way children would be raised, and not from him but from
Diana, he felt short-changed.

"My great-grandfather who struggled against the mythology of
his day, he'd be mortified to see me submit to the rites of Rome," he
told Diana.

"Well, we won't invite him," she answered. She did not want to
argue either, that would spoil everything, she said. He thought her
attitude toward the Catholic Church was somewhat akin to her
attitude toward *Vogue*.

"Concentrate on the real problem," she suggested. "Find us an
apartment."

"That I can easily deal with. It's impossible."

"My place is too small, yours is too, too everything. We'll have to
find a new apartment."

"Non quod sed quia absurdum."

"Exactly. Which means?" she asked.

"It means that the belief in finding apartments is the only kind of
mystery left for our times. It loses in translation."

"Are you sure you are doing the right thing?" It was a regular
question of hers. He didn't feel sure at all and he had the insight that

72

if he said "no" just then, that would be the end of the whole business right there.

He knew there had been a discussion about the possibility of a mass at the wedding service but he did not know the outcome; kneeling beside her in St Joseph's he was not certain what he was listening to. There was still much Latin and he let the words flow over him.

She looked amazing, he thought, in her off-white dress. Pure, as she had said. A bit puzzled. She couldn't be too sure herself of doing the right thing.

It was an extraordinary idea, to make a sacrament of this, a holy act; extraordinary to be able to take yourself and your fellow woman or man that seriously. Perhaps it gave a whole new weight and importance to making love. Or ruined it. He peered at the priest and noticed now that the man looked tired and distracted; he seemed to be stifling a yawn. Of course the answer to that would be that human shortcomings had nothing to do with the mystery.

A pleasant belief. One side of a coin. On the other side, the lethal self-righteousness of. . . .

I won't pursue that, not today for God's sake. Let's think about how this extraordinary ceremony may adorn our bodies when they are together in a bed.

The reception had people in two separate layers, one layer of Diana's colleagues and friends and one of friends of her mother's. Between the two, Balthasar's few friends floated: two men from the library, Andy Sheil (a school friend he'd kept up with), a girl who had been his girlfriend once and had remained a friend, and Miguel Ruiz.

The *Vogue* people shook hands with him while eyeing him with intensity as if searching for some hidden charm he must have but which escaped them so far. The friends of Diana's mother did not say much either, once they realized he was much too old for the kind of conversation they were used to with their friends' children. The men danced with Diana.

Miguel came over to him.

"You must not be bored at your own wedding," he said. "And with such a girl."

"Not bored. Lost maybe."

"Your mother-in-law is a very fine woman. She and I found much in common. We are both Third World people, you realize."

Balthasar raised his eyebrows.

"It surprises you? You think it is the colored nations only? The Irish, certain Spaniards, the Basques of course—we are all underdogs. The Jews, once—but no longer."

Balthasar smiled and waved at the setting, the vast room with its parquetry floor, the band, the waiters in black tie.

Miguel shrugged. "You know that has no meaning. I do not mean we're all poor. It means we see through the great hipocresía, the hypocrisy; it means we cannot fool ourselves we deserve this as you Anglo-Saxons do. We did not inherit this earth. We think no one did."

"Don't look at me, Miguel. I'm a Dutch heretic who got away."

XXVIII

Their departure went unnoticed. They let the car roll down her mother's driveway before they turned on the headlights. The road followed the dark Long Island Sound. Across the water, the lights of Connecticut were faintly visible through the mist.

"I know I'm a terrible dancer," was the first thing he said.

She did not answer; she seemed lost in thought.

"I do like music," he continued, "all kinds, even silly stuff. As a boy I used to know all the words. 'When the deep purple falls, over sleepy garden walls.'"

She smiled.

"Are you scared?" he asked. And then they both asked at the same moment, "Are you sure you're doing the right thing?"

"Red!" they shouted simultaneously.

"Hurrah. Make a wish."

Neither of them had any days off and they were to go straight back to his place, where they would live at least for the time being. He realized now he'd have to let her go upstairs alone while he was finding a parking space. Not very festive. "Let's stay away overnight," he said.

"All right."

In the frenetic Saturday night traffic he missed the Bronx-Whitestone Bridge. When he had finally reached the parkway to Westchester, she was asleep, her head against his shoulder. He drove as gently as possible, hardly moving his arm in order not to wake her. It was a long drive before he finally saw the exit sign where he knew a motel. Their room was warm and even quiet. They dropped their clothes, crawled into the large bed and fell asleep with their arms around each other.

The mechanics of their lives did not change very much. She had held on to her apartment, which she might be able to use in a swap. Sometimes when she worked late, she called and told him she'd sleep over in the Village. His place was bigger but it depressed her, she said, and they always ate out, either at the Cuban–Chinese or after meeting somewhere midtown.

He wondered what would happen in case she quit her job or he lost his. He did not know if she had stopped taking the pill; that was one of the things she refused to discuss. "You're still a very private person," he told her.

"Don't you prefer it that way?"

"Maybe a bit less. Otherwise, what would have been the point of that one-flesh—" He was about to say, "business" but switched to, "ceremony."

"But one flesh is not one mind. I think it means simply that our bodies are no longer our own, to do with as each of us might want. And you're a very private person yourself."

"Not by choice. I'm a very insecure person, really. You're my security, you know. My salvation, Dante would say."

She did not like that, she put on her unaccommodating frown, two vertical lines on her forehead.

XXIX

Miguel, who had postponed his return to Miami a number of times, showed up at Balthasar's desk in the library. "This is it, my friend. I've come to say goodbye."

75

"Oh, Miguel." Balthasar stood up. "I'll miss you. Did you finish the work?"

Miguel grinned. "I finished two weeks ago, don't tell my daughter. But now I really have to go back to her, poor creature. Here, for a farewell toast." He pulled a flask of rum out of the pocket of his rumpled jacket.

Balthasar went to get paper cups. Miguel poured, one for Susan; he went over to her and handed it to her with a little bow.

"Here is to you, John. I'll put you in the preface, you helped very much."

"Here's to your book."

They drank. "It's you who helped me, more than me, you," Balthasar said.

"We never talked about Amparo again, did we?" Miguel asked.

"You don't want to, do you?"

"No."

"Good."

"One thing, John. Don't trust them."

"I'll never have anything more to do with them."

"Good. Then I won't feel sorry I got you together with them. They have changed, my God, how they have changed."

"Well, forty years is a long time."

"Not long enough," Miguel said with sudden sternness. "Not long enough to serve as their excuse."

Balthasar did not pursue the subject. Dreams of a generation killed in that war or shot afterward. Forty years was too long. "You must have thought I was nuts," he finally said.

"Nuts? No, not nuts, my friend. A man of honor maybe, as we once used to call it in Spain."

They looked at each other, smiled, looked away. Miguel refilled the paper cups.

"Miguel, since your manuscript is all finished, why don't I mail it to Spain for you, from here? Wouldn't that be easier? We have a mailroom."

"It needs polishing. It needs a very clever letter to go with it."

"Well, how about me making a copy? They won't charge me for it."

Miguel considered that. "Could we do that right now?"

"Eh—we may have to wait our turn. It'll take a while."

"No, let's not. I'm carrying it myself."

"Call me if there's anything you need from this place, anything at all. Take care."

"You too, my friend, take care. And kiss Diana for me."

They embraced.

Two days later Miguel's daughter telephoned him from Miami to ask where her father was. He hadn't come back as he had promised and he was no longer at the Pickwick Arms. She sounded very nervous.

Balthasar tried to calm her. Miguel was in fine shape, very much better than when he arrived in New York. He might have stopped over in Washington to visit the Latin American Institute, for he had thought about that; he was enjoying his travels. ("His freedom," he almost said.) At that point Balthasar heard Diana's key in the front door. "I'll check with you tomorrow or the day after," he told the daughter. "Don't worry."

Diana came into the room and dropped into a chair. "A drink," she said.

He told her about the phone call. She laughed. "He doesn't want to go home. That was about the first thing he told me, that evening when I cooked dinner for him. Think how he's changed, he looks ten years younger, he's got rid of his imitation fur hat and of his funny accent. I bet you he's gone to ground somewhere."

"That's what I figured. I tried to tell her in a roundabout way that he hadn't been in any hurry."

But later that evening Balthasar suddenly said, "No. It is odd. He's a very considerate and a very old-fashioned man. They don't do things like that."

Diana gave him a glance and then turned back to the television. He picked up the phone and called Eastern Airlines. The records of completed flights were destroyed, erased, he was told. And when he insisted, a new voice came on and informed him that maybe they were kept but they couldn't be divulged. He was told to call back in office hours. Finally a supervisor agreed to consult a computer. She found a Michael Ruz on the noon flight of the day

Miguel had come to say goodbye. "That could be your party," she said. "Names get mutilated. I have nothing else that comes even near."

When he repeated this to Diana, she sighed.

"I wonder if his luggage—" Balthasar began. "No, he always carries his only bag, he carries it himself."

"Oh John, would you please let it rest? I want to watch this movie in peace. Do you always have to get yourself into a sweat about somebody?"

"I'm not a lunatic, if that's what you think. It was me who made him come here, you know."

"I see. And so whatever happens to him from now on is your doing, right?"

"You think it's abnormal to invite responsibility? Ask your Herr Doktor Katzenjammer—"

He stopped when she jumped up. "I'm tired," she said. "And fuck you, John." She left the room and slammed the door behind her.

He got up too. He looked out over the desolate concrete back yards; a solitary lamp was reflected in the puddles on which the drizzle made little circles.

Diana came back into the room and sat down on the old couch. "I'm sorry," she said.

"No, I'm sorry. I do go on."

"Yes, John. You do go on. And the name of my analyst is Doctor Helfrich and he was born in New York."

"I only meant that—"

"You're going to mention Dante now, I know."

He tried not to smile. "Camus, actually."

"What about him?"

"He wrote a novel about a man whose life is ruined because he doesn't save a woman, a total stranger, out of the Seine River in the middle of the night."

She sighed and made a face.

"Even *Vogue* would like Camus," Balthasar said. "Sexy French philosopher has Paris night clubs buzzing with conversations about Hegel. . . ."

"I never read anything like that."

78

"It was before your time. He's dead. He drove into a tree one day."

"Oh," she said. "I am sorry." And after a while, "You know, I really hate this room."

XXX

Balthasar found himself walking along a narrow street. Its uneven pavement made him stumble. It was the hour before sunset. He came to a small square and entered a squat stone building. Its corridors still caught the light through leaded windows; in the corners it was almost dark. But he knew where to go. He came to a hall, a small auditorium, where he sat down in the back. No one else was there.

A man entered the pit of the auditorium and busied himself with a trestle table and various objects Balthasar couldn't make out. It was like a science demonstration in college.

There was a long wait.

Two other men came in and they were carrying a fully dressed old man who seemed dead; they put him on the trestle table and then tied him to it with ropes, very casually as if they were tying up a carpet. This spectacle filled Balthasar with dread and he stood up to leave.

A priest appeared, dressed in a chasuble which shone as silk does. He spoke to the helpers, in a loud voice as if for Balthasar's benefit. Balthasar decided he must sit down again.

"This man has not been given any food for the past eight hours?" the priest asked.

The helpers shook their heads.

"It's of the essence to make sure of this," the priest said. "Otherwise the process will cause vomiting and asphyxia; that is, suffocation." Thank God, Balthasar thought, they're going to give the man an anesthetic. This must be one of those hospitals of a religious order which they have in Spain.

"We will begin," the priest announced. And said in a resounding voice, "Exsurge Domine et judica causam tuam!"

Prayers yet, before an operation.

One of the helpers had a long strip of gauze in his hand. He draped it over the mouth of the man on the table and as the other helper held the man's head, the priest started pouring water on it from a carafe.

Perhaps it isn't water, Balthasar thought, it may be something like ether.

The priest waited and then continued, a slow trickle now which pushed the gauze farther and farther into the man's mouth. Balthasar went down the steps of the auditorium and said loudly, "What are you people doing? Do you know what you're doing?"

The hands of the man on the table were clawing the air. "Will you speak?" the priest asked him, while turning his head toward Balthasar.

"We stop," the priest said. The two helpers pulled the gauze by each end. The entire length reappeared, darkly stained. One of them sniffed at the gauze and said something, and they laughed. The old man lifted his head up from the trestle table and Balthasar saw that he was Miguel Ruiz.

He took another step down the stairs and then thought, I must get help, I can't do anything alone. He turned and ran up the wooden steps and out into the corridor.

For a moment he seemed to have lost his way but then the heavy entrance door appeared, its iron gleaming in the last daylight. He came out into the street. It was evening, he saw no one, did not hear a sound. He looked left and right, wondering where to go for help. Turning, he saw chiseled in the stone above the iron door, Pamplona House of Mercy. A scream from the building woke him up.

XXXI

The magazine sent Diana to Chicago to attend the three-day convention of American fashion designers. He had asked her if she couldn't get out of it. That had surprised her; she thought he was jealous. But his reason was his sudden uneasiness at the idea of being alone at night. He couldn't possibly tell her that.

His first evening without her, he was late leaving the public library. The air was cold and windless, a thin moon stood in the black sky. The lights of the city seemed unnaturally bright to him. How nice it would have been to meet her in some nearby bar or walk up the avenue with her and look in the shop windows. He had the feeling he had already taken her too much for granted and had not appreciated the potential of their life together. But we've only been married for a month or so, there is very much time.

It did not reassure him. Why does being together with her seem so fragile, he wondered; after all she has pledged herself in an absolute way. It's more than most men and women do nowadays when they draw up their reservations and conditions before they've even started. Fragile, and yet pedestrian too. No, not pedestrian. *Usual*.

He looked into people's faces as he walked on. They must be happy, very much so, pleased with themselves. Fragments of animated conversations reached him. Those who were by themselves had expressions on their faces which said, we're not lonely, we're on our way to meeting someone. Or if we're not, it's by choice.

Several of the gold and jewelry stores were still open; two bearded young men could be seen at a counter, discussing an ornament and painstakingly both weighing it—as if it mattered, as if they were their grandfathers in some small Polish or Russian town of the year 1900 instead of now, a *now* in which the students of Brown ask their school to lay in a supply of cyanide pills, enough for everyone if there is an atomic war. HCN, that consuming scorpion built out of such innocent parts.

He turned the corner of Sixth Avenue and squeezed himself on to an uptown bus just as its doors were closing. But he could not move once he was inside and after the driver had passed two stops and then halted on Broadway, Balthasar jumped off again. He saw the name "Ciro" on a restaurant, he remembered sitting on its terrace with Diana one summer afternoon. He went in.

It was too early for the dinner customers and only a few tables were occupied. "I'm waiting for someone," he said and ordered a vodka. At the window, a youngish man in a business suit, with a heavy gold bracelet on his right wrist, long black hair, very dashing, sat beside a girl with shoulder-length straight blond hair; those two were staring into each other's eyes, touching and laughing, and

81

taking only distracted bites from their plates of pasta. The waiter refilled their glasses from the wine in an ice-bucket but they paid no attention to him.

I don't trust them. They aren't really absorbed-and-aware-only-of-each-other. They're acting out for themselves, if not for their scant public, how glamorous young people have a rendezvous in a New York restaurant.

Just then the girl moved her head; her eyes went around for a moment, rested on Balthasar. There was no smile on her face then. She is checking the scene, she's off camera. Too much has been shown, it has ruined us. Not me, but that is because I am really out of it. I'm ten years older. My childhood is from before. Before some great deep divide.

Stop. Maybe they're doing all right, maybe it's me who's ruined. Maybe all those images and examples, that steady stream of models they have, is precisely what keeps them going. While I on the other hand am steadily heading for the madhouse. I'm a man trying to live like those before me, say, like my mother, but I have to do it without her security, without any example applicable to my time. They are new and so they live like the quote celebrities unquote they watch so much, though not of course as those celebrities really live. As their reflections, smiling, chatting, determined, unconcerned, safe, politically neutral, no, neutered. *Successful.*

He had a number of vodkas but when he opened the dinner menu and saw the prices, he went through a little pantomime of looks at his watch and at the door, and left. He'd eat a hamburger on the way home.

He walked up the avenue and peeked into coffeeshops and foodshops but did not go in anywhere. He noted with some satisfaction that he was slightly drunk. Dark and light streetblocks succeeded one another, the light blocks with shops and restaurants, much chromium and unpainted wood, photographs of smiling women, the dark ones with barred windows, blind walls, and scattered among these the surviving shoe repairman, Chinese laundry, newspaper shop. A tramp was lying full length in a doorway, his breath visible in the freezing air. Young men in leather and in camouflage jackets like mercenaries watched Balthasar and appeared to be indifferently weighing whether to kill him or let him go by.

I'm imagining things; their eyes simply follow moving objects just like the eyes of a cat. They don't see me.

He arrived at his building and hesitated before going in. He felt a flash of disappointment. With what, with having reached his destination unhindered, alive?

He went upstairs, double-locked the front door behind him, and sat at his window without turning on the light.

The telephone rang. Diana, he thought, and his mood changed totally. For a moment he stood still in the middle of the dark room, for the duration of two rings he waited and wondered how a phone call from a woman could change the way the world presented itself to him from sad to happy. So much for cosmic despair.

It was not Diana. The call came from Miguel's daughter in Miami. She announced in a wooden voice that Miguel had been found killed, in a car parked along the Tamiami Canal, not far from the Miami airport terminal.

XXXII

Diana did not call that evening or the following day. He did not know where she was staying and resentment built up in him. He visualized her at parties in Chicago while he was sitting here by the telephone waiting, needing to talk about Miguel's death, afraid to go out and miss her call which did not come.

The third evening, lying on the couch and staring at the ceiling (he saw for the first time that it wasn't plaster but badly painted hardboard), he heard the elevator stop at his floor and then her key in the lock. He sat up with an angry face.

She came in, put her suitcase on the floor, and fell into a chair. "Why—" he began but when he saw how tired and pale she looked, he stopped his sentence.

"Jesus," Diana muttered and she closed her eyes.

He smiled reluctantly. "Poor Diana, you're all in."

"I am."

"Too much partying."

"Oh boy, I wish it was true. I was in bed every evening at nine."

"You weren't sick, were you?"

"In a manner of speaking."

He instantly knew what she meant. He stared at her.

She gave him a weak grin. "Morning sickness," she said. "With me it's midnight sickness, hours of it. I'll never forget the decor of my bathroom in the hotel. Shepherdesses with parasols, yellow ones. The shepherdesses."

He stood up and went over to her and touched her hair for a moment. "Take your shoes off. Come, lie down here. I got tea bags, do you want a cup of tea?"

She nodded.

He stayed unnecessarily long in the kitchen. He reappeared with a mug of tea and she sat up on the couch to drink it. "You're not overjoyed," she told him.

"I just haven't yet—they've been miserable days here, too, a kind of vacuum, hoping you'd phone. Why didn't you?"

"Oh John. I didn't want to talk about it on the phone, and I was in no mood for chit-chat. I had all I could handle, doing the work they wanted me to do without anyone being any the wiser; I sneaked off to bed as soon as I could. They must have thought I had a lover in Chicago."

"I see. I understand. Sorry."

"It wasn't all bad, there were some nice times, yesterday's lunch when—I'll tell you later. I'm okay during the day."

"You're sure then."

She nodded solemnly. "Sure I'm sure. I was sure before. It's that he or she decided to start acting up. On the plane out. It doesn't like flying."

He smiled.

"I'm happy with it," she said.

"Me too."

"Have you eaten?" she asked.

"No. I was waiting."

"Let's—What you got here?"

"Nothing really. Let me go get some take-out stuff at the Cuban. Can you eat that?"

84

"Sure."

"I'll be right back."

They ate in silence for a while and he thought, I have to do better than this. "I *am* pleased," he said. "Honored is the word, maybe, that you want a child with me."

"But?"

"No buts. Or, well . . . You know, Monday, I walked most of the way home, I missed you, I felt sort of vulnerable. I went across to Sixth Avenue on one of those jewelry-store streets, you know—"

"And?"

"It was cold and dark but some were still open. I stood there watching through a window, two men, orthodox Jews, young but all in black, with skullcaps, looking like rabbis, they were discussing a brooch or something, with such earnestness, first one weighed it and then the other—"

Diana now looked hard at him, apprehensively.

"—and I thought, why do they bother so, why do they take it so seriously? They act as if they were still in their grandfather's world or their great-grandfather's world, the security of the year 1900, some little town in the marches of Eastern Europe, their grandfathers must have handled their affairs that way even if maybe they weren't weighing gold but chickens or potatoes—"

"Security of some little town?" she asked. "What on earth are you talking about? Security of the little towns of their grandfathers? Haven't you heard of pogroms? The Cossacks used to ride through those little towns, they had the Black Hand, they'd cut off the head of every Jew they could find. Those two young men were survivors."

"I know," Balthasar said. "And it wasn't the Black Hand but the Black Hundreds."

"Well what are you talking about then? And what has it to do with your wife being pregnant?"

I shouldn't talk about this. Not now. "Cossacks with swords is a threat on a human scale," he finally answered. "Terrible but still the sort of threat people have coped with for thousands of years. You can think about it, you can hide, you can outwit it. Those two men had, that is to say, their great-grandfathers had."

"I want to know—"

He interrupted her. "It wasn't a threat to the weighing of gold. On the contrary, gold outwits it. It did not vitiate the world. It's not the same as living now."

"Vitiate," she repeated, her voice going up sharply. Then she opened her eyes wide. She stood up and turned her head away, and he was certain she had started to cry.

"I didn't mean . . ." he muttered.

She avoided looking at him but went into the bedroom and he heard her lock its door.

XXXIII

Oh damn. Why did I go on like that, why, why *reveal* this? I was sure I would not ever do that. But I didn't really know what I was going to say, did I. And here she is, tired, and pregnant, and all the rest. Poor girl.

But of course her pregnancy is what this is all about. Our making a child. When the odds are that all our children will die, singed to death. Am I not supposed to consider that, shouldn't I have been consulted? A bottle of vitamin C's for the expectant mother. Put in some cyanide pills too, miss, just in case.

She had already been sure before going to Chicago, she said. How long before?

He stared at the cartons with food, at Diana's chicken-and-vegetables which was still almost full, her chopsticks standing up in it. He went to knock at the bedroom door.

Her muffled voice, "Go away."

He sat down again, took some bites, then picked up all the cartons and threw them in the garbage bin in the kitchen. He poured the tea out and started washing the cups. Over the sound of the running water he heard her unlock her door. She appeared in the doorway of the kitchen.

He put his things down. "I'm so sorry," he said. "Please forgive me. I exaggerate. There's no earthly need for you to share my obsessions. My hang-ups."

He had never seen her like that, pathetically waiting for some reassurance, it seemed. There was a frightened look in her eyes, red from crying. Think of those press screenings of ours, how she looked then. Young New York career woman. Jesus, have I done that to her.

He put his arms out but she stepped back. "Well," he said, "I'm alive, I haven't considered killing myself so who the hell am I, telling some poor creature it'd be better off not born. There are a million babies born each week or each day or whatever, so we may as well have our own."

"I hope you mean it."

"I mean it."

"It's too late now, anyway," she said and smiled.

"Yes. How late? I mean, how far—?"

"Three months or so."

"Three months!" He considered that. "You mean, we had a shotgun wedding?"

She laughed now, and shook her head. "Not really. I was quite ready to have a baby by myself."

"Your Church—"

"I have my own definitions of sin."

"But you'd rather be married."

"I'd rather be married," she agreed.

He was confused. I must figure this out, he said to himself. Was that the reason she suddenly wanted to marry me, or part of the reason? Was I quote honored or tricked? That Sunday morning when I thought she looked so ethereal. . . . Well, either way, I guess I'd better let it go right now, we've had enough for one day and it's ten o'clock, too late to get a divorce tonight. He didn't know why but now he felt good. Diana was kneeling beside her suitcase and came up with a bottle of champagne. "Stolen goods," she announced. "Is it all right to celebrate?"

"Yes. Yes, of course!"

"And I can tell my mother?"

"Absolutely."

"I'm hungry," she said.

"Oh shit, I just threw the food out."

She looked in the bin. "It's okay, I'll fish it out and heat it."

*

They were lying on top of the bed. It was very warm in the bedroom, he wanted to get up and try to turn off the radiator but he couldn't quite make the effort. Diana had expected to get sick again but she hadn't; she was sleeping on her back, peacefully. "Making love must be good for it," she had said. And as often when he looked at her sleeping naked, he was overcome with amazement that a young woman would trust him, would entrust herself to him like that, sleeping, nude and vulnerable. It was beyond the act of making love, even of marriage.

He put his hand on her belly, careful not to wake her. It would be too unjust, he thought. They are not going to blow us all up.

Then again, why would there be justice?

Or turning it around, why wouldn't it be just? Suppose it is precisely the final come-uppance for all of us here, retribution for what we've done to the rest of the world. The Third World.

Miguel. Christ, I never told her.

Maybe as well. She needs shielding now.

From me, mostly.

XXXIV

The following day two FBI men showed up at the library "to ask a few questions about the death of Miguel Ruiz".

He asked why the FBI was involved.

The two, one older man with thick white hair, one improbably young in appearance, consulted each other with a long look. "Does it seem far-fetched to you," the older man asked, "to assume a Cuban angle to the case?"

"Yes, it does. Seem far-fetched."

"We don't think Mr Ruiz was killed for his possessions. His luggage is missing but his daughter states that its value was nominal."

"His bag—is his bag gone?"

"Yes. Why is that important?"

"It means his manuscript is lost, he worked on that for years."

"Can you tell us what it was about?"

"Not Cuba, I assure you. Nothing political."

"Please let us be the judge of that, Mr Balthasar," the young man told him.

"Oh for God's sake. A literary manuscript, about Basque letters."

Look at those faces, those contemptuous pseudo-polite smiles. But of course, they could damn well be right, not about Cuba, but who'd want to kill old Miguel unless it was one more death in that civil war of fifty years ago? Lucas, the changed man, as Miguel had said. Amparo with his mercenaries.

He opened his mouth to tell those men about Amparo's army but changed his mind at the last moment.

"Yes, Mr Balthasar?" the young man asked quickly.

"Nothing. I had an idea but it's nothing, I was wrong."

"Let us be the judge of that."

"I tell you, it was nothing."

"You were in Spain last summer?"

"How did you know?"

The young man asked, "You do want your friend's murderer found?"

"Yes. Of course. Do you?"

"How are we to understand that question?"

"Well, if you're right, if this is political, then the murderer or the murderers are people of the right. For Miguel was a Basque, he was against Franco, he was and is—I mean he was—a—oh, never mind."

"You think we approve of the killing of radical Basques, is that what you are trying to say?"

Balthasar shrugged. Why don't I shut up. He answered, "I'm not *trying* to say anything, I said exactly what I meant to say. Doesn't our government, doesn't Washington, let the Miami Cubans and all those other guys run wild?"

"And where did you get that information? What do you base that surmise on?"

"That surmise? It's in *The New York Times*. Every day."

A silence.

"Are you yourself a political person?" the young man asked.

"I'm against—No, I'm not a political person."

The FBI men looked at each other and got up. "Here's my card," the old man said, "in case you think of something that could help."

He did not tell Diana about that visit, but when she asked if there was news of Miguel, he had to tell her Miguel had been killed. She turned very pale.

"How was he killed?" she asked.

"I don't know." He realized the daughter hadn't told him and he had not thought of asking her. What difference did it make. Found near a canal, close to the airport. He could visualize the scene, fences, garbage, shuttered and abandoned gas stations—the landscape of death.

The water torture. The dream, the priest in the chasuble. Didn't he have a face seen before? Lucas? Martinez? Oh fuckit, this leads nowhere. I've got to stop this. I must not end in a straitjacket.

"John," she said softly. "You look half-sick too. Let's not think about it any more, not tonight."

What I can do, he thought, is to try and save his manuscript. I must find it. That would be a propitiation of sorts. If it gets published, his life will not have vanished without a trace.

XXXV

A box of microfilm was waiting for him on his desk. He knew that was a record of purchased material which he had to catalogue. He got up to go and look out of the window. All he could see was a dirty strip of sky. Dull blue, framed by zinc gutters. The roar of the city buses swept across that sky and drained it of its last color.

He opened the bottom left-hand drawer and brought up his 1802 Dante. *His*: he had never sent it to the binders. No one had ever asked about it. He felt that he needed it more than any possible reader and that therefore what he had done wasn't particularly wrong. They'd fire him if they found out.

He did not even understand this Dante universe with its numbered mountains and roads, human doors and staircases in the heavens, its systematic thought, but he knew that it wasn't naive, it was a mystery. The writer had given sense to everything for the love

90

of a woman and of God. He wondered if there were still descendants of Dante living on this earth.

Balthasar could no longer learn easily by heart, yet he tried to memorize the lines in Italian. Each canto had been printed in English and Italian both. "Susan, listen," he said. His colleague across the room looked up.

"Susan, I must read you something, okay? Just one line. Okay? 'L'amor che move il sole e l'altre stelle.' That's the last line from 'Paradiso'. Each book ends with the same word, 'stars'. It's all like a building, a construction. 'The love that moves the sun and the other stars.'"

"It sounds like a song from a musical."

"What? Oh for God's sake. Oh well, maybe it does. But not when it was written. It was new then. Burning new."

"What are you doing there with Dante?"

"Cataloguing."

"Oh. Yes John, I can see now how it was beautiful once."

She was a friendly girl.

He phoned Lucas and found him at home. "Hello Mr Lucas. This is John Balthasar."

"Eh—oh, yes, of course. We wondered if we'd hear from you again."

"About Miguel Ruiz."

"I was sad to read the news."

"The police have been here to interview me. Not the police, the FBI."

"I'm surprised. Do they have any clues?" Lucas did not sound very interested.

"They didn't say. I wonder if I should suggest to them to see you also."

That sentence was the best Balthasar had been able to think up in order to test Lucas, to see if it would make him nervous.

It did not. "If you think it's a good idea—not that I have anything for them. To be frank, not long after that little party in his hotel room, he and I had a difference of opinion and we stopped seeing each other. I wrote once or twice. No answer."

"Really? And here you were such old friends." Balthasar tried to put doubt or irony in the words.

"Yes. Regrettable. Mind you, it wasn't me disliking him afterward. He was a good man, but he hadn't matured so to speak, in all those years. It was tiresome to hear him come out with those same half-baked theories, half a century later. He was really a child. Very sad. Killed just like that. The crime of our cities. A lottery."

When Balthasar did not answer, Lucas went on, "Did you call me for some special reason?"

"Yes," Balthasar answered, "I called because Miguel's manuscript vanished, the one he had worked on for so long. I felt that maybe his old friends should try and find it, offer a reward perhaps. There's the publisher he had in mind; his daughter would know. It would be like a, well, yes, like a monument for him, wouldn't it. It would surely help her cope with it. It's such a waste, otherwise."

"John, I think that is a very fine idea. I really do. As I said, I never stopped thinking of him as a friend. You can put me down for a hundred dollars of the reward."

"You don't have any suggestions how to go about it?"

"Let me think. No, not really. As I told you . . . The daughter, she's your best bet. You talked to her already? The daughter, and the Miami police. It was a literary work, not very useful to a mugger, is it. A reward may do the trick, but it will be a matter of luck. It may be sitting in someone's garbage can."

"Yes, I guess so."

"Right. Now you know where you can reach me, John. Come by for a talk one day. I mean it. Don't wait too long. Don't be a stranger as they say."

"Thanks. And I'm at the library, the 42nd Street one, extension 0811."

"I'll remember. Good luck with the manuscript."

Well, I guess he's just being polite. Memorizing my extension, he sounded as if he meant it. Look at Susan slaving away there, she's the future of this department, that's for sure, I'm the past. But my Dante goes with me if they chuck me out. I wonder if they inspect everything when you leave for the last time? Not very gentlemanly. But then of late this place begins to look like the Pentagon anyway, locks, metal gratings. Perhaps someone is watching me right now on some little screen.

He stuck out his tongue.

Where would I land a new job? And Diana will have to quit eventually or we'd have to hire a nanny or someone who'll then earn more than I do now. Diana will never get used to 104th Street, she wouldn't want to. She'd leave me first.

What's ahead of me beyond her? The drab run of life. "The unbearable half-sleep of life." Or is it "the bearable half-sleep"?

The idea of her walking out of the 104th Street place unnerved him. But why the hell hadn't she—she must have been taking pills once, mustn't she, she must have done something? How strange if she believed that's a sin against God. Not strange, more than that, unbridgeable. But she tries to be pure. As people once did. No matter how it is defined.

Puro e disposto a salire alle stelle

As very long ago.

Going home he had to let three packed buses go by. On the next one he got a seat in the back beside a heavy man in a leatherette jacket and a baseball cap who took up most of the space. After some squirming Balthasar said, "Do you mind," which his neighbor answered by mimicking his words and then adding, "I fucking well do mind."

"Oh shut up," Balthasar said.

At West 96th Street the bus emptied considerably and he moved to a seat across the aisle, but when he got off at West 104, the man came out after him and put his hand on his shoulder. "No one tells me to shut up," he announced.

"Well, I did." Balthasar knocked his hand away.

The man produced an old-fashioned folding knife with a wooden handle and opened it with deliberation. "I'll give you three seconds to get on your knees," he said.

Pedestrians stared at them in passing but no one stopped. Balthasar discovered he wasn't really afraid; that pleased him. Could he possess courage of sorts? But how could he not run away? Have his life ended over a bus seat? What a mess.

It wasn't cold but an intermittent almost invisible rain dampened his face.

"Come on, man," a black teenager yelled at him from across the little park on the divider. "Kick him in his balls, he's all fat."

93

The man with the knife turned around at the kid. Balthasar stayed immobile for one instant, then he turned and walked away. I won't look back, I'll go slowly. That will be enough of a test.

When he had reached the front door of his building and looked up the street, there was no one there. He felt the sweat run down his back.

He had to tell Diana about this but he'd make it sound funny. They were sitting in the Cuban–Chinese restaurant. As he told her about the fat man, she stared beyond him, toward the door.

"He isn't going to come in," he said. "You know, it was an affair of honor. The West 104th Street version of a duel."

She wasn't listening to him. "We have to get away from here," she told him.

"There are men with knives everywhere."

"I had a lead," Diana said. "I didn't bring it up, I knew how you'd react." She looked down at her plate. "You'd say, 'We can't afford it', right? And that you like living among the people, right?"

He was about to answer, "Right, we can't. I can't. Sight unseen." She was still avoiding his eyes and her face had turned red. He said to himself, shut up, you're undoing this girl, why don't you shelve your principles and Calvinisms.

"No, I won't say that," he answered softly. "If that's what you need, that's what we have to do."

She gave him a radiant smile, the kind of smile she had when he just knew her. "No kidding," she said. "All right then. It's a two-year sublet. Midtown, or almost. West 68th Street. I've a good chance, there's this man at *Vogue* . . . Anyway . . . You're sure now?"

"Sure."

"How you frightened me. With that story of the man on the bus, I mean. You didn't know, did you? You don't know much about me yet. But now I'm glad it happened."

"I didn't mean to frighten you. I wasn't frightened. I know I should have been. To be or not to be. No that's wrong. To be or, or nothing. You can't have a subject to not-being, can you. Well, I only afterward broke into a sweat. Maybe that's a dividend on my contemplations of the end of the world."

"What? What are you saying?"

94

He hastily shook his head. "Nothing, never mind. My private *angst* as they would say at your magazine."

"They would?" Then she surprised him by adding, "It would have been the end of the world for you all right."

"Not the same."

"And why not?"

He shrugged. Keep still, lie low. "Did you get home on the bus?" he asked her.

She shook her head. She usually took taxis and felt defensive about that, especially just then after he had given in on moving. She earned twice as much as he did.

"I'm only asking," Balthasar said, "because the service was all screwed up tonight. Worse than usual. People shoving, how they all hate each other. You'll say New York is a jungle but in jungles each species has solidarity, don't they? If this town is a jungle, then every single person is one species by himself. Or herself."

She put her hand on his. "How you go on," she said. "And how you frightened me."

XXXVI

She telephoned him at the library: "I've got it. The apartment! Wait till you see it!"

She sounded inordinately happy. He was glad he had not tried to stop her.

"I'm taking the afternoon off," she said. "Will you come over after work? It's 32 West 68th Street, the top floor. Will you be surprised!"

He found her in a large empty room with two bay windows, talking to a man wearing white overalls over a business suit. "This is Ed," she said. "He's going to help me fix the place."

"What needs fixing?" Balthasar asked but she ignored that and led him around. There was nothing in the rooms but scraps of carpet and wall fixtures of wrought iron from which electric candles with imitation wax drops spread their light. In the bathroom a tap shaped like a winged dragon released a trickle of brown water into a small tub on carved legs.

"Isn't it gorgeous?" she asked when they were back in the front room where Ed was making a list on a piece of paper he held against a door.

"Yes . . . Very big."

"Of course it needs work," Diana said, "but Ed has promised to do me first." She took Balthasar to the window. "Don't worry," she whispered. "We have to pay some key money, but I'm going to ask the same for my place in the Village."

"But if you only have this place for two years . . ." he began.

"I'll get a new lease, don't you worry. Once you're in you're in. Right, Ed?"

Ed looked up, holding his list which seemed very long. "What's that, Miss Heffernan?"

"I said to my husband, once you're in you're in."

Ed confirmed this.

A different routine began. Diana was in fine spirits now; she went to the new place after work and showed up late on West 104th Street with her scrapbook and more lists, and plaster dust in her hair, and ate without complaining whatever he had cooked. Balthasar felt that only now did she look married. Modern virginity ended by finding an apartment.

"I don't want anything from here," she told him. "Give it to the Salvation Army."

"You're kidding! My desk, my bed? What's wrong with them?"

She shook her head. "If you don't know . . . Well, try and sell them if you must. You're really too old to go on living like a hippy."

"Like a hippy? My mother, when she was fifty, would have liked—" But he didn't pursue the point.

Diana was tireless now and no longer bothered by any nausea. When she came into the bedroom at night after having washed off all the plaster or paint, her wet hair in a towel, she was more beautiful than he had ever seen her. She must have been aware of that herself and pleased with it, for she walked around naked, a thing she wasn't used to doing.

Her breasts were even higher and there was a deeper curve to her belly. He thought he had never seen such a curve. He thought of that statue of Venus in Naples which a guide had shown him in a locked museum room after some winking and palming of a tip. There was nothing scabrous about it, it was just overwhelmingly erotic. The statue was called the Callipygous Venus, he had been told, the Venus "with the beautiful ass," the guide had whispered. With the beautiful cunt. It was not a name you could forget. That was in stone, Diana was like that in flesh.

XXXVII

Lucas's hundred dollar check arrived. Balthasar did not recall what it was for until he saw written on the back, "For the Miguel Ruiz reward." In the same envelope was a check for a thousand dollars, signed Captain William Willers, Amparo. These men were still loyal to Miguel then, in a certain way—unless they simply wanted to show they had nothing to do with his death. No letter came with it, only a piece of paper, "As agreed. JL." The paper had an embossed seal, two concentric circles with in the center a cross, a sword, and a tree branch. Between the two circles were some printed words, too vague to be readable. So now Lucas has a coat of arms, Balthasar thought, just like Captain Rivers of the Spanish coffee shop.

He tried to telephone Miguel's daughter in Miami from the library, always a lengthy process because long distance calls had to be approved and billed to the caller. There was no answer. She must have gone back to her job, he thought. Or suppose she is sitting in that empty apartment and answers neither the phone nor the doorbell, suppose her life is shattered and I haven't done a damn thing to help. But think of all those folks at the Pickwick Arms. After all, Miguel must have had older and closer friends than me here. He wrote her a letter instead, offering his help and enclosing the checks. He told her how he had admired her father and hoped she might salvage her father's manuscript, with the assistance perhaps of the Miami police.

She telephoned him back in answer. Her voice was sad but no longer with the lifelessness of her earlier call. She'd do anything to save her father's work, she told Balthasar, but she didn't know how to go about it. The police were unhelpful, "fishy" was the word she used, and when she had called them about the reward, some man at headquarters, he had not even given his name, had said, "No one bothers for less than five to ten grand, lady." Maybe Balthasar could come over later in the month, and see? "They'll be different with you, you know," she said.

Well, no, he had no free time, and no money.

"You could use some of the reward money on it," she suggested.

That night he began his dream once more. He returned to the Pamplona House of Mercy and watched the priest pour the water which pushed a strip of gauze down Miguel Ruiz's throat, but before the dream could go any further, he forced himself to wake up.

He put some clothes on and tiptoed out of the bedroom. His face was burning; he was glad when he was out in the street and felt the wind and the rain on it. It was just getting light.

I must straighten this out. This tenuous connection of torture and justice within me. Pain is a mystery, I imagine I'm not afraid of it but I don't know it. What baffles me is how it's generated within your own mind and yet you don't seem to be able to stop it if you're not an Indian, or a fakir. It is strange because it is a movement without a lever outside your own body, it's pulling yourself off the ground by your own hair. Inflicting pain, torture, is the greatest crime because it is outside nature. That man, what was his name, so-and-so Levin, Michael Levin, who wrote in *Newsweek* about the legitimacy of torturing political prisoners—he put himself outside the natural world. Perhaps that is what hell is about. Evolution did not take torture into account, could not anticipate it.

Or, who knows, evolution is going to avenge all our victims through all our history by having us develop to that precise point where we are able to wipe ourselves out and do so. Then all inflicted pain will be equaled and surpassed by our broken-down world in which everyone is burned to death by fire and radiation. That would balance the bookkeeping. Evolution doesn't take individual cases into account. In the end life returns into its track. Human beings like dinosaurs did not work out.

The bedroom in Huelca with the bleeding Heart of Jesus on the wall.

He ducked into a coffeeshop. Two men were at the counter, reading the *Daily News* and eating large helpings of eggs and

98

home-fries. The cook scraped the top of his stove clean, lit himself a cigaret and smoked it in the doorway with visible pleasure.

The freshness, the equally mysterious freshness of a new day. I must go to Miami and help the daughter. I'll ask for compassionate time off, a death in the family, they never refuse that. And Diana won't mind, she'll be too busy to worry about it.

XXXVIII

From the escalator descending into the lobby of the Miami airport building, he immediately saw Miguel's daughter. She looked so much like her father that for one dreamlike moment he imagined it was Miguel dressed up as a woman, reversing the scene of his own arrival in New York, come to welcome Balthasar, to reverse the wheel of time.

She had spotted him too, came toward him and said "Mr Balthasar? John?" in a loud, unmodulated voice.

"Yes." He blinked, took a deep breath. "Sorry—the plane—I was in a bit of a trance."

"I'm Elsa. I recognized you right away. My father has a picture of you."

"He did? Does?"

Her voice was low, without any Spanish accent. She was an old woman; the label "daughter" had had a connotation of someone young for Balthasar. She was stout and swarthy and ugly. Miguel's dark and heavy features certainly did not become a woman.

She had an envelope in her hand which she gave him. "The plane fare, John. I want to settle that right away. No, don't worry about it, it's from that reward money. And you know, the bus isn't that much cheaper. I mean, I don't mean that you would have had time to. . . ." Her voice died out and she stared at her shoes.

"Miss Ruiz, you know how very sorry I am about this."

She nodded.

They came outside and stood under a pale blue, early spring sky.

"I have my car here," she said and pointed toward a parking lot.

They did not speak as she unlocked its doors, carefully put on the seatbelt and her glasses and drove out on to the highway.

"Where to, John?"

"The police, no? The fishy cops. I had a telex sent from my office, from the public library in New York. About my arrival. It doesn't mean anything, but it gives it a bit of an official push."

She gave him a startled look before turning her attention back to the traffic.

"A little trick really," he added. "The kind of thing you get used to doing when you're a freelance journalist."

"Oh. Yes."

He couldn't think of anything else to say to her just then and she appeared content to stay silent. He observed her and thought how different she was from what he had imagined and how much the odds were against achieving anything in a two or three day visit. But then, it would have been even more difficult not to come.

He had put a shirt and tie on in the morning instead of his usual turtleneck sweater in order to impress any officials. But he felt he already looked disheveled and badly shaven. It had been too warm on the plane, and it was too warm in her car.

Sooner than he had expected, Elsa turned off the highway and pulled up at a big brick building, modern but with an air of neglect. She drove past the entrance, stopped, and turned to Balthasar. "Do you want to go in with me or alone?"

Before he could answer, a policeman rapped on the car window. When she had rolled it down, he said to her. "No estacionar aqui, muchacha."

Balthasar answered for her. "Vat, officer? Ve speaky English."

"Visitors' parking around the corner," the man said and walked away.

"He wasn't so bad," she said to Balthasar.

They went in together. At the desk Balthasar showed his old press card and said he had come in the matter of Miguel Ruiz, and that he had sent a telex from New York.

"You want the Media Relations Office," the desk sergeant told him.

"No, not really. I was a close friend of Mr Ruiz. This lady here is his daughter."

"Media Relations Office. Down the stairs, on your right."

At the stairs, Elsa hesitated. "Sorry," Balthasar said. "I didn't

100

handle that too well. But we may as well go there first now."

"They're dealing with, with my father's case, in the homicide bureau."

"I realize. But you said they were fishy."

"Fishy?" Her face came to life. "They were—pigs. There is no other word, John, excuse me. The man there, he never even gave me his name, he asked, 'Lady, you know how many Hispanics get wasted in this city every twenty-four hours?' Wasted, he said. And then he asked if my father had been into drugs."

"Jesus. What did you say?"

"I walked out."

At the Media Relations Office they penetrated to an official who had received Balthasar's telex and now reread it a number of times. Balthasar told him that Ruiz had been a prominent literary figure, well-known to the research staff at the New York public library, and that his daughter had not been treated very considerately. The media man for some reason avoided looking at Elsa but he made several phone calls and then told them a captain in homicide, a Captain Elk, would see them at ten the next morning.

No, it was impossible to see him that day. "And I wouldn't bring the lady," he said to Balthasar in an undertone. "They get too emotional."

He and Elsa were standing outside again. How mild the air is after New York, he thought. She gave him a look, so hesitant, afraid almost, that it hurt him. He smiled at her.

"It's a long drive to my house," she said, "but do you mind a ten-minute detour?"

"No. No, not at all."

He didn't recognize the landscape but she seemed to go back toward the airport. They went down an empty road paved with large blocks of concrete, at their left decrepit little shops and houses, to their right a strip of yellow grass, a wire fence, and a canal of dark water with rainbows of oil on its surface. She pulled over. "This is the place. This is where Miguel was murdered."

Balthasar did not speak, he only shook his head.

"Or better, where he was found," she added.

He got out of the car and stood in the dry grass. The wind was strong and smelled of petroleum.

Elsa came to stand beside him. "Shot through the head," she told him. "No time for contrition."

"He was a good man, I didn't know him that closely but I knew him a long time. You need not worry about contrition and forgiveness of sins."

"But you're not a Catholic, are you, John." She did not say it as a question but without thinking he answered, "Actually, I am."

"Are you? Will you pray with me then?" She bent her head and muttered a prayer; he wasn't sure but he thought it was in Spanish. She glimpsed at him and he closed his eyes and folded his hands. Old Miguel, you were a tough bird, tougher than I am. Less given to belly-aching. I don't think you'd mind your kind of death, a bullet through your head. Perhaps when you are a Basque you are mad enough or brave enough to think that's a proper way of dying.

Back in the car, after a long silence, he said, "It's odd, here they tried to tell you it's just one more Miami murder. An old friend, a former friend, of your father's also tells me it's street crime. But two guys from the FBI came to see me in New York and they were in on it because it was supposed to be political."

"My father did not want to live here," she said by way of answer. "He was not happy here. But imagine, his newspaper, after all those years, they gave him about a hundred dollars a month. I tried to keep a good house for him, I have a good job, well, good, it's okay, I save money."

Yes, Miguel had sure been far from home, Balthasar thought. See these mean streets. "How did you happen to end up here?" he asked her.

"I was going to get married, to an American. But then I didn't. It is *very* old history."

By the time they got to her house, it was almost dark. She turned on the light in the narrow hallway, and then opened a door and turned on another light. "Miguel's room," she said. "We have no spare room, do you mind sleeping in it?"

He saw that she had tears in her eyes, and he bent over and kissed her on her cheeks. "No, I am glad you'll let me."

She cooked dinner for them and showed him album after album of photographs.

"I loved him very much, John. I was so glad when he decided to come live here. In a way it's my fault."

"Oh please. He loved you too. I'm sure he was happier here than alone in Pamplona."

"Love me? Perhaps. But he didn't like me very much. He liked pretty women."

He was glad to sleep in that room. No bad dreams.

XXXIX

Captain Elk was a polite man, dressed not in uniform but in a neat dark gray suit. The file was of course kept open, he immediately said to them, but to be perfectly frank (How I hate that expression, Balthasar thought. Ever since Nixon), he could hold out little hope for any quick developments. "In crimes of this sort—"

Balthasar interrupted. "What sort is that?"

"The sort—"

"Mr Ruiz was a distinguished man of letters. The fact that he spoke Spanish as his mother tongue did not make him a dope pusher *per se.*"

"Mr—" The captain looked on the appointment card they had brought in. "Mr Balthasar—"

"Captain, this man, this man of letters came to our country to live with his daughter. On the pension he had earned in his own country. Some sergeant or lieutenant in your section told his daughter that it was hardly worth the trouble to keep track of all the wasted Hispanics."

"That is to say—" Elsa began.

"You're being flippant," the captain said to Balthasar. "And raising your voice in here will do no one any good. Miss Ruiz, what is the name of that officer who is alleged to have spoken in such a way?"

"I'm glad to say I never knew his name."

"We don't take murder lightly in this city. There is nothing in the file to suggest that Mr Ruiz's death was taken lightly. You must have misunderstood the man."

"That's it," Balthasar said. "It's your fault, Elsa. If you'd only learn to understand English."

"It does not matter," she answered in a low voice. "John. It is not very pleasant for me to sit here and listen to you and this gentleman arguing. It may help you. It doesn't help me."

"I'm sorry," Balthasar muttered.

"What we want," she went on, "what Mr Balthasar came here for, is my father's travel bag. It had nothing of value for a thief, but it had a manuscript he had worked on for many years."

The captain leafed through Miguel's file once more although they had already seen it contained only a few forms, one red, the others white, with some typewritten lines on them. "There's nothing here about luggage of any sort. A wallet, keys—All these have been handed back to you?"

She nodded.

"Part of his file still seems to be at the mortuary. At the crime lab. These papers take a long time getting back to me. I will give them a ring. I'll call them right now." He tried several numbers without getting an answer. "They're very busy there—Are you both staying in Miami?"

Oh no you don't, Balthasar said to himself. "Can't we go there ourselves, Captain?" he asked.

The captain appeared relieved at the suggestion. "Sure. I'll give you a note. It's in the Jackson Memorial Hospital, do you know where that is?"

"I was there last week to identify Mr Ruiz," Elsa said. Her voice was almost inaudible.

"Of course, of course," the captain answered.

Perversely, the people at the mortuary were downright jolly compared with those at police HQ, but after some tos-and-fros it appeared that the man in charge of the Ruiz file was in court. He'd be back at two.

"Oh God," Balthasar said very loudly. "At two, are you sure?"

They were sure.

Elsa left her car in the parking lot; they found a restaurant a few blocks away. Its customers were policemen and suspicious looking types whom Balthasar first took for defendants—the court building

104

was around the corner—but then realized must be detectives, for everyone was shaking hands and cracking jokes.

He sat in a booth with Elsa. Outside the window the urban landscape consisted of clapboard houses and an abandoned and broken-down gas station; an uninterrupted stream of traffic went by. "You know what," Balthasar said, "Why don't you wait here. Let me go alone. If you're needed, I'll come and get you."

He thought she'd refuse but instead she smiled, for the first time. "Thanks," she answered.

It was only twenty minutes to two; he slowly walked back to the laboratory. The sky was of the same tender blue as the day before, but he felt a great, tired sadness mastering him. It'd be simple to say it's because of Miguel, he thought, but it's more than that, it's not that. I could almost believe I'm jealous of Miguel in a way. Maybe the just are privileged to die, before the final horror.

The man he got to see was young, thin, in a white coat, his office chaotic and full of ringing and unanswered phones. "I'll read you my report," he said right off, "Miguel Aragon Ruiz—born 1899 —alien resident permit etcetera you don't want that stuff—cause of death presumed one bullet wound in the—time of death, January 28, 1984, between midnight and six a.m.—bullet .32—thirty-twos are as common as cigaret lighters in Miami—Here's an odd bit: his stomach containing two quarts of water—"

"You mean they could have drowned him?"

"No—the lungs were clear. I honestly don't know what it means. I've heard of mafioso double-dealers being forced to drink, to make 'em spill the beans, but that's liquor, and anyway this man was no professional, that's clear. I just don't know. There's always things you'll never know. Effects, one suit—and so forth and so on. It's all been checked now. Result: nothing."

"And there's no bag? A traveling bag?"

"Wait. Yes. In the back of the car. Sure. Papers, laundry."

"You're joking. At headquarters, they said not."

"It's checked off."

"Well, fuckit. Can we have it?"

"I don't see why not. Except that it says here you got it already. His daughter did. You sure she hasn't? Okay, okay, I'll call the stock clerk."

An hour later a man came to Balthasar in the waiting room, carrying Miguel's bag. It was torn; a rope had been wound around it. "You can't sign for it," the man told him. "Not if you're no relative."

"Oh damn—I'll be back in five minutes. Don't lose it again!" And he ran off to get Elsa.

Miguel's bag. They put it in the back of Elsa's car and drove straight to her house. When Elsa got it open, papers, socks, handkerchiefs popped out. "That's the police's doing," she said. "My father was neat."

She went to get a laundry basket and put all the clothing in it. There wasn't much. "He did his laundry every night in the hotel room," she told Balthasar. "I'm going to put this in the machine, you start sorting out the papers."

The manuscript was there. Five hundred and seven numbered sheets of typing paper, covered with Miguel's tiny handwriting. There were also two dictionaries, and cards with notes, some letters. A diary for 1983 with the New York months empty. A menu—it was the menu of the restaurant where he and Miguel had eaten their dried-out veal on the night of his arrival. Miguel's reunion treat. Why had he kept it, could he have looked at it as a souvenir, of a memorable occasion? God, I have disappointed this man somehow. Have I failed him?

Elsa came back into the room. He could feel the little house vibrate with the washing machine. "Is it all there?" she asked.

"All there. Amazing. It was so easy."

"I wouldn't have gotten it out of them."

"But of course. Of course you would have."

"You know, John, I get angry too. But different from you, I can't show it."

The letters were mostly those she had written Miguel in New York. There was a note from Lucas (Balthasar recognized that embossed stamp), which said, "Miguel don't be a fool. For old times sake," and signed, "J". She handed it to Balthasar. "This one sounds like a threat."

"It's from a guy who was once your father's friend but turned against him. His name is Julian Lucas."

106

"Sure?"

"Sure. That's his coat of arms or whatever he thinks it is. He sent a hundred dollars, remember?"

"Oh." She shook her head. "No, this Lucas wouldn't make threats. I know he was bothering my father, Miguel complained about it in his notes to me—he wrote me a little note every evening, you know. But no threat, Lucas thought Miguel was a child and that he had to tell him everything. Lucas once contributed one chapter to a book, about our civil war. Ever since he was an expert. He was showering my father with advice. Miguel said it was as if he had been waiting all those years just to do that."

"You sure there wasn't anything more to it?"

"Who's ever sure? What I know is, my father made fun of him."

He refused to let her drive him to the airport. They called a taxi. When they heard its horn, they both stood up; she turned quite pale. He knew she would have wanted to ask him to stay longer, but neither of them said more than, thanks, and goodbye.

XL

He sat in the back row of the almost empty plane, Miguel's manuscript in his lap. In the inside pocket of his jacket he discovered an envelope: Elsa's money for his plane fare. He had forgotten about it and on the strength of it he ordered a Scotch from the stewardess. A beautiful girl with copper-red hair. Imagine an airline with call girls for stewardesses and a special little compartment where you could take your turn. There'd be an outcry but business would be terrific. Or maybe businessmen precisely prefer it like this, through a glass wall. I haven't given a thought to Diana in the past two days. That is risky. I'm one-half married to a very real young woman having a real baby this year, and one-half paralysed or obsessed by a future which is imaginary.

Or is not. Suppose that future is reality and the father-to-be in his normal world is imaginary. He is normal, he does an honest day's work, just like the crew of this plane, just like those busy detectives in the restaurant where Elsa sat waiting two hours for me, staring at her slowly curling piece of apple pie. Vital work. What could be

107

more vital than these folks working to get us down safely at Kennedy and when we're down, it isn't a happy ending after all, for all of us will perish none the less, as miserably or more so. He in his car, she in her bed, wherever, and not in the fullness of time. Well before. Stop, Death, eternity, that is all I have to say to myself. Two words. Finally, it-does-not-make-a-difference. The little scorpion built of nitrogen, carbon, hydrogen.

That lady, where was it, some bar on West 12th Street, she told me the proof of immortality was that people have energy and energy is never lost. It was around the corner from 12th, on Sixth Avenue, she was waiting for a class at the New School. Is that what they taught her there, pseudo-science? I'd rather have her pray to Saint Jude. But I'm glad, glad for her that I didn't contradict her. Let's think about Elsa for a moment more, before she vanishes below the horizon. At some point she stopped being an ugly woman I didn't know and stepped into Miguel's shoes. A friend. God knows she needs a friend but what can I do about it, nothing. Nada. She'll be back at work anyway. Back at work she'll have to stop crying.

Anyway. Anyway, here's Miguel's book. One decision kept. With no meaning in the light of etcetera etcetera but meaningful within the frame of today.

When he walked into his room at the library, Susan greeted him with a thumbs-up. "He's sort of nervous about your absence," she called out to him. "Good you're back. Maybe you should check in."

"He" was Mr Oliver, the head of administration, who had looked sour about his compassionate leave. I'm not going to report back in like a high school kid.

He took Miguel's manuscript to the reproduction department and as soon as a machine came free, he started Xeroxing it, which took two hours. Then he took it to the mailing room where he wrapped it. Elsa had written a note to the publishers to go with it, a house in Barcelona. They hadn't given Miguel a contract but were supposed to be committed.

He had to sign for almost forty dollars of postage but he felt a surge of relief and peace when the mailroom clerk dropped the parcel in his airmail bag.

While he was at the copy machine Diana had called, Susan informed him. He was on the verge of calling back but then decided, no. I'm going there, it's early, I'll pick her up. She'll find me waiting.

Miguel's souvenir veal-dinner menu he put next to the phone on his desk. As if a family photograph.

When he had his coat on, he decided to call back Mr Oliver, but was told the man was in a meeting.

At Grand Central he bought a dollar bouquet of roses and walked over to the *Vogue* office on Madison Avenue. It was only just after five.

Well-dressed young women came out of the elevators in numbers and their eyes swept past him without touching, a radar which was automatically turned off when meeting an unshaven face or a crumpled shirt collar. There was a kind of rock garden in the lobby of the building and when he sat down on its low brick wall, the doorman immediately walked up to him and announced, "Can't sit there, Mac."

"Says who?"

"Says the owner."

"My name isn't Mac and—" but the man had gone.

Oh the hell with everyone. Let's get away from here.

An elevator door opened and he saw Diana come out within a big group and when it dissolved, two men and a girl walked on with her, deep in conversation. He decided, I'm not going to show myself. But as he hesitated, she turned her face in his direction. Its expression changed completely, her little smile became radiant. She said something to her companions (who looked his way and then continued out the revolving door) and hurried toward him.

He stepped back and held out his roses. "Sorry I look so shabby," he said. Then he had to smile at her.

She kissed him. "Am I ruining your I'm-sorry-for-myself act?" she asked.

"Yes."

"I'm glad to see you, I can't help that."

"Why, for God's sake? Look at me."

"Terrible. But the Father of my Child."

They went to the Cuban–Chinese on Broadway. He told her about his journey, Elsa, the police, and Miguel's book. She reported on

109

the progress to her new apartment. It was Balthasar who had started calling it *her* apartment, as if to avoid the responsibility, but she had followed suit.

"So Miguel was taken for a ride," she said. "That was no mugging, was it."

"There must be something in the air now, in the air of this country I mean, which makes those old Franco guys feel very much at home. Free to do what they feel like. Like, revenges."

"You know, before my father's death I had never known any person who then died. Before Miguel, I never knew anyone who got killed."

"Well, me neither, I don't think," he answered.

He still had Lucas's note to Miguel on him and showed it to her. "Isn't that spooky, that seal? Like a coat of arms or something."

"Spooky?" in a very high voice. "Be your age, John. Why spooky?"

"There's something unpleasant about it. If not sinister. Like some Ku Klux Klan type organization."

"If it's on their stationery, they aren't very secret about it, are they. Anyway, we weren't ever going to mention those men again."

"True."

She was still looking at the note. "It's a Latin motto of some sort. I can read 'causam' here."

"That's all right then, classical spookiness. Is that really all you want, spaghetti?"

"Yes. Lent started today."

"Those rules aren't for ladies in your condition," he said.

"How did you know that? I know I don't have to do this. But I have my private reason, you see."

"Very private?"

"Yes."

Later she said, "I'll tell you if you want to hear it. I feel lucky, you see. Privileged. I had worried so, and then things turned out well. I need to make some little sacrifice now. I know it sounds silly."

"No, no. Not at all."

Oh God. She was actually blushing. Lucky. A sacrifice.

XLI

The library had a heraldics expert and he showed her the embossed seal on Lucas's note. "Possibly the Pentagon," she said, "Or more precise, the DOD, Department of Defense." He found a number of listings in the New York directory for that department and called its General Information, its public affairs officer and finally the "Commander", but if anyone who answered knew about a departmental seal they considered it classified information.

He phoned Lucas and told him the manuscript had been found. "There was a note from you among the papers," Balthasar said and added what the heraldics lady had told him.

"She's right," Lucas answered. He sounded impatient. "I worked at the Pentagon as a clerk after I'd left active service. The sword and the cross, I liked that emblem. And no, no threat, for that's what you're implying, isn't it? Ruiz refused to go and see a literary agent I knew, he preferred doing it his way, getting the run-around from some newly emerged ex-Red Barcelona publisher. And no, I didn't have him murdered for that."

The moment Balthasar put his phone down, it rang. His boss, Gene Oliver, expressed surprise at the business of his line.

"I'm trying to trace a lost book. Misplaced by the binders, I think."

"I see. Something precious?" Oliver was more friendly now.

"No, not too. A nineteenth-century Dante. I'll find it."

"I see. Well, glad you're back. I hope it all worked out."

"It was a sad occasion but. . . ." Balthasar let his voice trail off.

"Ah yes. We must have a serious talk soon, you and I. There are problems. Not today, I'm frightfully busy too. I will call you next week."

There we go, I bet you. Expectant father gets the sack. Jesus. And an apartment, a rent coming up five times what I'm paying. Why don't I stay in at lunch time, leave the door open. With luck he'll walk by and see me at it. Catching up, Gene, sir.

It was a sunny and mild day, however, and after twelve the corridors stayed empty, everyone seemed to have gone out.

Balthasar took his Dante and read and reread lines in an Italian of which he understood only bits and pieces. It haunted him. Not as a book, he was aware of that. As a talisman.

He went over to the closed shelves of the Rare Book Room; he wanted to look at some of the early editions, wanted to hold them in his hand.

A 1477 Dante, printed in Naples, name of the printer unknown, was catalogued. A 1502 edition printed by the famous Aldus in the first italics ever used, based on the handwriting of the printer's friend Bembo. But they weren't in their places. A Venice edition —it wasn't there either. Instead he found little wooden planks, labeled like imitation books, a pseudo-library like those pasted on the doors of liquor cabinets. He took one to the duty clerk, a youngish man in a shetland sweater, shirt and narrow tie whom he knew by face only, and who was having a lunch of orange squash and a Danish.

"What is this?" Balthasar asked.

"Don't you know? Haven't you seen these before?"

Balthasar shook his head.

The clerk shrugged. "It's no secret, though we don't talk about it too much."

"Well, for God's sake what does it mean?"

"Those are very special and precious books, they've been evacuated, to some cave in the Rocky Mountains, I think. Some can be sent for, in special circumstances, but then they go back again. It's a big nuisance."

Balthasar had turned pale. "You must be joking! They must be fucking joking. You mean they're ready to blow us up and then the survivors, a couple of senators up from the Congressional bomb shelter maybe or else some new human types a million years from now, they'll still have our italic Dante to write some fucking thesis about . . . ?"

The duty clerk was embarrassed by Balthasar's outburst. "Come on now," he said soothingly. "Don't take it like that, it's only a civil defense routine. Now if you really have a need for the Aldus Dante, there is a special form which—"

Balthasar walked away.

Yes, I have to keep my shirt on, he urged himself, I can't afford to get pegged here as a freak. Still, if Manhattan and Diana and her baby get atomized I want that fate shared by Dante. He would agree with that.

If he could conceive of it. But of course he could not. Imagine, that crystal world of his of concentric spheres with the saints watching us, and watching Mary and God, with people doomed for sins like greed or venality, and if someone had predicted to him that those creatures on the inner sphere would have the power to atomize that whole structure! Such a prediction would have driven the poet insane.

As it should. We too should not be asked to contemplate that. We cannot. The scorpion.

Later that day he went back, told the man in the shetland sweater that he was sorry, and requested some of those special forms. And from then on he started applying for one evacuated book after another, using names of different foundations and projects. It worked more often than not and when they came, he put them back in their old places and threw out the little substitute planks.

XLII

He worked late, too, in case Mr Oliver was stalking the corridors, and it was quiet on Forty-Second Street when he came out. It was that indeterminate hour between people going home from work and going out, an early spring day which had now turned chilly. At Sixth Avenue the corner lay deserted. Its streetlights were out at two places and it was dark there.

He went to sit on a bench in the little park; lightless, soundless, like being in this city long ago, before all this began. All this what? I'm not certain. If I close my eyes, perhaps I can think myself back to those dark and green days. But it may have been more natural for them to think forward than for us to think backward: wandering here through the forest covering Manhattan some of them must have had an inkling, a vision, vague perhaps, of incredible noise, a torrent of stone and iron. A vision of horror and deaths. Perhaps they had magic to stave off such visions.

The magic does not work.

113

They kill you in this park. Not then, now. He heard a bus approach and hurried to the stop.

At West 104th Street, the table was set and Diana was waiting for him with drinks. "Guess what," she said, "this is our last meal in this dump, it's a celebration, we're moving tomorrow! I got the morning off and I've got a little man with a van lined up who's going to help me."

"That's nice, darling. You've done all the work, I'm afraid."

"I wanted to. I hope you're pleased. You're not just pleased for me, are you?"

"No! I'm no masochist, I'd rather be on 68th Street too. I'm not helping anybody by living here. It's only that—"

"Yes, I know. Don't say it. And I've got something else for you, and you've got to accept that too. Promise."

"Well, tell me what it is first."

"Promise first."

"Okay. What?"

"I got you an appointment with my analyst. With Clyde Helfrich. Please, John. Everything is so nice, I don't want it to get spoiled, and you look terrible. Come on, you promised just now. Just have a talk. He's expecting you at five tomorrow, he's giving you the first cancellation which was very nice of him. And after that you come home to 32 West 68th Street."

She looked very pleased with herself.

How can I help you? the doctor asks. Well, sir, I have these unpleasant dreams.

Hmm, unpleasant dreams, eh? Bad childhood? Bad digestion?

Well, sir, neither, really. But maybe life itself is an unpleasant dream.

At ninety dollars an hour, young man, we do not encourage our patients to come up with their own diagnoses. In fact, the rules of the American Society of Psychiatrists forbid—

Oh screw. What do I know. Perhaps the man can help me. Perhaps I'm simply suffering from a morbid condition of my thoughts or memories or conscience. And I promised her.

"Does it cost ninety dollars an hour?" he asked Diana.

"Yes. But don't worry about that now. Tomorrow is on me, anyway. Try it."

114

Walking up Park Avenue toward the doctor's office, he was overcome with a feeling of unreality. How had he reached this point? How did a rather impoverished last descendant of Balthasar Bekker, minister of Christ, come to walk New York City's Park Avenue, the most expensive street in the world maybe? Was this a way to get the family name refrocked? Or, to think of a more recent Bekker, to repay the disinherited tribes of the Fox and Sauk? Rubbing shoulders with these glass buildings where the riches of this world were collected and then redistributed, redistributed without mercy?

Still and all, it's my home as much as anyone else's. He studied the people on his sidewalk. No, it is not. They are more at home than I ever was, it shows on their faces, as much on the faces of those guys in the gray suits and powder blue shirts who control the wealth or anyway sit in the same room with it as on the face of that hot-dog man who maybe doesn't speak English yet but who came here straight as an arrow and knows damn well why he's here and who he is and where he is. And here I am on my way to some office of sandalwood and beige carpets and prints of, who? not Van Gogh for sure, he ended up in the madhouse, bad publicity, of Warhol maybe, or something abstract or perhaps just a No Smoking sign, to assert and pay for my right to be happy and tranquil and at peace.

The days were visibly lengthening. When he crossed the side-streets, some last flashes of the setting sun reached him and touched him. He came to the building where Helfrich worked, he looked through the glass at its doorman who stood in the lobby, yawning. Then he hurried on, he fled as if that doorman might come after him and drag him into the doctor's office, until he reached a coffee shop on Lexington Avenue where he sat down on a stool all the way at the back.

XLIII

But Diana's pregnancy began to make a cocoon for both of them. She said she had moved into the West 68th Street apartment just in time. She pulled the drawbridge up behind her; once she was home from work she wanted neither to go out again nor to see people. She was naturally enough focusing on herself and appreciated what she thought was his readiness to stay with her in that isolation. She did not know that he himself needed their "going into hiding", as he called it.

A subdued sense of peace. The library administration and its Mr Oliver seemed to have forgotten his existence. Nothing to remind him of the past few months but Miguel's souvenir dinner menu.

Diana now had a sense of vulnerability about her own body and was afraid of making love. It fitted in with his mood; he felt no desire for her then. She looked very well but her body had at one unknown moment gone beyond that mysterious curve of the Callipygous Venus. For a brief time it had been of a superb, classical, beauty and eroticism; it would never be that way again. (If she had been aware of that, she might have secretly regretted that no one had seen it but John Balthasar.) She now looked what she was, a healthy young American woman having a baby, an event which eventually might spoil her figure. None of this had any bearing, though, on Balthasar's feelings. His sensuality had turned in upon itself and was as sterile as the desires of a young boy. Diana felt she had to make up for what she thought she was depriving him of, and when she came to bed she would often pull the covers back and pet him. He liked to watch that and came very quickly, aware only of his own body.

She had furnished the apartment in a way suited to the building itself, which had gone up in a mixture of styles with a limestone façade. She had bought modern pieces but also taken solid old stuff from her mother's attic, easy chairs and sidetables which reminded Balthasar of the houses he had grown up in, the early ones. After his parents were divorced, his mother had had to move to a small and dingy place, and ever since he had believed and proclaimed that he did not "believe in possessions".

They had only lived in their new apartment a week or two when he came home one night to find a little note: Diana's mother was in town and had picked her up. She'd be back early.

It was just after six o'clock. Three, well perhaps four hours to get through, he thought. He did not want to do anything specific, he paced through the rooms and stared out of the windows. It was the first time he was consciously alone in the place. Only now was he aware of its shape, a square-cornered, fat letter C, facing south, on the eighth floor. Maybe eighty feet above the pavement, say a hundred feet above sea level, above the oceans, no view of anything really but walls and blank windows and a tree. Little traffic noise. In the small room at the far end of one of the arms of the C, a room Diana used for storage, he could hear the machine of the elevator. It must have been a maid's room once. It had a kind of trap in the wall, a dumbwaiter perhaps; he tried to open it but it was stuck fast.

He visualized the city, transparent, celluloid, and this one apartment colored red or black, pinpointed in space, between a park and a river, facing, not south, southwest by south it would be, facing the setting sun in winter if a path were cleared through all those buildings down to the ocean shore.

Ten million people. Take a mortality of ten per thousand, that means a hundred thousand New Yorkers die every year, three hundred a day, twelve an hour. Say half of them in hospitals, or on the streets; six an hour die in cubes or prisms or parallelepipeds such as this one. I would have thought it was more, much more. But ten million waiting in those boxes.

It was only just after seven when he felt himself glide into panic. A dream? A dream about flies.

After a moment's hesitation he went to the front room. It held a chair such as his mother had once owned, of dark polished wood, short legs, a leather back. He carried it with an effort to the maid's room. He had to push a pile of cardboard boxes aside to get it in, then he closed the door and sat down in the chair, letting his hands glide over the brass studs in the arm rests. He closed his eyes and listened to the sounds of the building. They were few; the whine of the elevator; muffled, far off, the slamming of a door; an indefinable cry as from a child.

After a while he began to calm down.

When he heard the elevator stop on his floor, or that was how it sounded, he jumped up and started lugging the chair back to the front room. When he was still in the hallway with it, Diana came in.

"Hello," she said. "What are you doing?"

"Nothing. I was trying out something."

"I'm bushed. I'm in no shape for traipsing through a department store. Mother insisted that—"

"Are they open that late?" he interrupted.

She looked at him with surprise. "Some, till nine."

"Oh." He picked up the chair and carried it to the front room, banging against the doorpost on his way.

That night he dreamt of Spain again. But this time he seemed to retain some sort of control; he saw the Pamplona House of Mercy, then Huelca, and it was as if someone was showing him color slides. He steered away from places he did not want to see and chose the Madrid bar.

He could not see the girl, but the bar itself he saw clearly, the counter, the basin with the dishwater, the arms of the barman. Behind it a spotty mirror with picture postcards stuck into the edge of the frame, postcards in violent greens, blues, and reds. At the top of the mirror it said in matted letters, LA DULCE SIRENA.

XLIV

At the library the following morning he went straight to the North Reference Room and pulled out the two books for Madrid from the foreign telephone directories. There, in its place, was a Dulce Sirena, *bar*. He had not doubted it. He looked up the listings for hotels and found a Hotel Europa. If he remembered right, that was the name of his hotel, the hotel where he had never slept, a couple of blocks away, and its phone number started with the same exchange as the Sweet Siren.

Now what? A note to the barman of the place. "I'm trying to get in touch with a regular of your bar, a girl in a yellow dress with red flames on it. Young. Missing two or three front teeth. She works out of a nearby apartment, next to a pharmacy. Please send me her name and address, it's important."

He went to find the boy who had brought him the Bekker book. "I need another note translated into Spanish. Will you help me?"

The boy read the draft and began to laugh. "No, no," Balthasar said hastily, "It's not what you think. No long-distance hanky-panky."

"But it's fine with me, doc." The boy looked at him with interest. "But this girl, has she only one dress?"

"What? Oh, I see what you mean. Never mind, leave it like that."

Balthasar retyped the note in Spanish and enclosed an envelope with his name and the library address on it. Then as an afterthought he put in a ten-dollar bill.

He got up, to take the letter to the mailroom, and sat down again. I'm repeating mistakes, repeating a cycle of dreams, opening a new can of worms. On the other hand, I'm not crazy. This is unfinished business and no Valium or analysts can finish it for me. I need advice.

Why not ask Andy, he's a neutral observer. It will give me something to talk about.

It so happened that for once he was to meet a friend that evening. His old and, maybe, only friend left, Andrew Sheil, who had been to the wedding and sent a wedding gift, had called to invite them a couple of times. Diana wanted to stay in but she had insisted he'd go. He was going to have a drink with Sheil after work, at P. J. Clarke's. He decided to hold on to the letter and let Sheil tell him whether to mail it or not.

Balthasar got to the bar early. He had walked over, planning the way he could tell the story without sounding odd. He went through the bar-rooms but did not see his friend. The place felt inimical to him. The bearded young men at the bar frowned when they thought he might come and sit next to them; waiters made sure he didn't take any table. He asked a barman, "Could you take a message for a Mr Andrew Sheil?"

The man shook his head, "Don't know him," and turned away.

To hell with this place, I have to get out of here. Tomorrow I'll apologize to him. He hastened out, afraid now to bump into Sheil at the last moment, and did not slow down until he was two blocks away. I won't go home, he said to himself, Diana would be upset, I'll take a bus ride downtown. He walked over to Second Avenue.

At the bus stop corner stood a mailbox. He hesitated, his letter to Madrid in his hand. When he saw the bus approach, he dropped it into the box.

He stayed on all the way to the Bowery, a long ride with a driver who made a point of missing the lights. When he finally got off, the streets lay deserted under a sky losing its last glow. He made for a neon sign but it was a cleaner's, not a bar. He turned a corner into the increasingly derelict neighborhood and found a bar, a couple of men watching television, a dark room with a row of empty tables under pink wall lamps which weren't lit. He took a table and ordered a double bourbon for the pleasure of hearing himself say those words.

Presently he felt better. Nothing wrong, he decided, with dodging out of a date at the last moment if you didn't feel up to it. He remembered the gentleman friend of his mother's fleeing through the back door if there were visitors he didn't want to meet.

And this kind of place really suited him better than P. J. Clarke's. Straight and simple, not very dirty really. A barkeeper whose face showed a kind of grave respect for the human condition, for men who respected their drinks and needed them. None of that arrogant gentility of uptown here, no kirs and spritzers. Spritzers. A dark street whose name he did not know. Les mystères de New York. Perhaps this bar was called The Sweet Siren, a good name for a bar. Perhaps that black-haired girl in the doorway was the girl in the yellow dress, led to this place at this day and hour by an endlessly meaningful, endlessly baffling providence.

The girl in the doorway became aware of him looking at her and entered. She was in a dark-blue raincoat with the collar up but even so he could see she was not the girl of the yellow dress. She had no teeth missing; she was haggard but young, too. She walked up to his table.

"Is this chair taken?" she asked in a low voice.

He shook his head.

She sat down. "Buy me a drink?"

"Okay."

"What are you having?"

"I'm having bourbons and branch water. A whole slew of them."

"I'll have the same."

She tasted her drink and asked, "What's branch water?"

"Tap water, I guess. I'm not quite sure. It sounds good."

"Oh." She gave him a little friendly smile. "You're from out of town, aren't you?"

"Not really."

120

"I'm to wait here for my mother," she said.

"Your mother?"

"Yeah. She's difficult. You can't cross her."

A long silence. He ordered another couple of drinks.

"You can do business with her," the girl said. "She's a business woman all right."

"Yeah. I'm sure." Being pimped by your mother. Poor devil, she had some color in her face now. Anyone who'd show her some sympathy, surely, could help himself to whatever pleasure he could get from that belly she was in charge of. The only thing in the world she was in charge of. Could help himself for free, too, in spite of mom. "Let's have another one," he said.

She put her hand on his for a second. "My turn. This one's on me."

"Absolutely not. Eh—"

"Tom is his name."

"Tom! Two more."

"You're out of work, aren't you?" she asked.

That surprised him. "How did you know?"

She smiled, pleased with herself. "I know men."

He put his fingers through hers. "You've got nice hands," he said. "You sure bite your nails. How do you get that deep?"

"It's better than smoking. Cheaper too. Here comes ma."

"Oh. I'm off."

She held her head sideways. "Come back some evening, why don't you. I'll tell mother you're an old friend, she'll make a deal."

"Okay."

"Thanks for the liquor. Be sure now. Any evening."

"I promise."

Out of the corner of his eye he had seen a heavy woman lingering at the bar, probably hanging back in case she'd spoil a sale. He avoided looking at her as he went up to pay his bill with Tom.

On the bus back home he thought, I could have asked her name, she'd have liked that, and I don't know the name of the place either. Still, I guess I could find it again if I had to. Had to, what am I talking about? I'm pissed. I'll have some coffee on Broadway. I've got a dollar left.

The multiplicity of lives. Is that a word? Why not. Let's say her

121

name is An—Anna. Anna, I say, I've fallen for you, come with me. We take a bus out west; I've got some money in checking, she'd steal back whatever mom has potted away somewhere; change in Chicago; just after dawn we stop in some little town we like; we get off.

He saw them walk in the early light along the quiet, foggy street to a motel near the bus terminal, he carrying her plastic suitcase. The kind of shower stall they have in cheap motels. Screwing. She'd moan and wriggle the way she'd been taught, and then yawn heartbreakingly. Still, nice, sort of, bony for sure, hip bones sticking out. Sleep. Hamburgers in the coffee shop. You folks need work?

Work somewhere, live somewhere. A barebone existence, precisely as you see in those thirties New Deal photographs. A totally physical life. Not so bad. A life outside the movement of time.

XLV

His self-addressed envelope enclosed in the letter to the Madrid barman came back to his desk so quickly and unexpectedly, that he stared at that address typed by himself and wondered what it was. When he realized, he did not open the letter but put it in a drawer.

And I didn't even mark it airmail, he thought. So much mail gets lost, our office mail with zip codes and the whole business, crazy that this worked. Well, I asked for it.

At twelve he went to find the stack clerk to ask for his help with translating but could not find him. He took a Spanish–English dictionary back to his desk instead. There was going to be no need for that: he opened the letter and thought the barman had sent him back his own note but then saw written at the bottom, in pencil and in English, "Sir. I know the girl. Andrea. Very nice girl. Sorry, she is dead. She dies in fire. Your sincirily, Arno."

Balthasar blinked, stared, his heart beating very loudly. But it didn't really say that, did it; the words were scribbled with a thick pencil, he could see how the man wet it between his lips; perhaps it did not say "in fire" but something quite different. He put the note back in the envelope and resealed it with tape. He went out into the corridor with it where a guard lent him his matches. He entered the toilet and burned the letter over the bowl, dropping it at the last moment and flushing the ashes away. I'll simply forget this, I can't puzzle over what it said because it's gone. That was a good move, a good way of coping with it. I do not need an analyst to help me recall things, I need a confessor to help me forget. Perhaps I'll ask Father Martinez if a non-Catholic can go to confession.

He sat back at his desk and had his hand on the telephone when he saw a man in uniform approach.

"Yes?" he asked.

"You can't get away with this, John," the man said.

"With what?" Was it me who murdered Miguel?

"No, you can't. Give me back my matches."

Holy Jesus. I better go home.

XLVI

He asked Diana about confession. He thought that might please her but it didn't. "Helfrich is your confessor," she answered. "You do see him?"

"Yes. Sure." I must explain to her, some other time.

"It's almost Easter," she said. "Confession used to make me feel so happy when I was a young girl. That's no good reason for it, I know. I'm not sure any more what I believe of it. It would be lovely if it were all literally true."

"Not lovely for the rest of us."

"Perhaps what you really believe, that's how it will be. Perhaps everyone gets what they expected."

Continuity of ideas. Or, the same fear we all try to escape from. "You know what," he said, "Horace, the Roman and Greek poets, they aren't in Limbo as some kind of punishment but because they had not been able to imagine something more glorious. That's in Dante. They got what they expected."

A vague smile from her. "We can go to confession together," she told him. "They don't ask you for your papers, you know. You just say, 'Bless me Father for I've sinned.'"

"Bless me for I've sinned? That makes no sense. What does it mean?"

"That's what you say."

"Anyway, I want to confess to the sins of others."

She frowned. "Are you serious?"

"Yes." But seeing her expression, he hastily went on, "No, no, of course not."

Easter was spent with her mother at Northport. On Easter morning, a few minutes after Diana and her mother had left to go to church, he jumped up and went after them.

He had to walk but it was not far. There was singing and no one paid attention to his coming in. He sat in the last bench but he could see the heads of Diana and her mother up front. He had thought the church would have been more crowded.

Much white and gold, bouquets of lilies, and ushers in pearl gray suits coming by with the collection plates. Just like my wedding; there is no link or continuity between these friendly routines and the Church when it was a Great Power, arrogating its Great Power right to torture and kill.

He slipped out and sat on the steps in the sun until the service was over.

"Happy Easter," Mrs Heffernan said to him. "Christ has risen."

"Happy Easter."

"I'm taking you two to lunch at the club," she announced. "If you can stand a lot of screaming kids rolling Easter eggs."

He walked a step behind them on the narrow tiled path through the grass leading to the church parking lot. Diana had put her arm through her mother's. They were both wearing white hats. Those two have taken me to their hearts in a way; I'm quite enviable walking here, on this clear sunny day, in this clean community where everyone smiles at everyone, today anyway, about to have lunch in a light sunny room with waitresses in white uniforms who will also smile and ask, would you care for a cocktail, Mrs Heffernan. He was fighting a mounting dread; there was a roaring sound in his head. He swallowed hard, more than anything frightened that they would notice.

An image of his mother, trudging up the steep incline of Joy Street. Little Boston streets dirtied by all those dogs shitting all day. Gray silent Sundays. She would have deserved—he had thought —All too late. For ever.

When they got to the car, Mrs Heffernan had to search in her purse for the keys. He had no business, no solidarity with these two women. He furtively wiped his face. The roaring ended. Diana patted his arm. "Poor John, were you very bored?"

In a dark wood. Mi ritrovai per una selva oscura

XLVII

"Confession by a person not a member of the Church would not lead to absolution," Father Martinez said. "At least, that's my first response. Of course, if the person admits to not being a Catholic, the priest wouldn't offer the absolution."

"But chuck me out instead," Balthasar suggested.

"I assumed you weren't talking in the abstract. No, he wouldn't chuck you out. He'd offer you instruction."

"But *not* admitting it would actually be a sin under your dogma?"

"Dogma, dogma—No, I don't see how it would be a sin, not if your intentions weren't evil. And who can say what happens between a penitent and God? You know, John, all these finer points of scholasticism or legalism are not of great interest any more. They are not what it's at, if you permit me the expression."

"And what is it at?"

Martinez gave him a hard look and then his eyes wandered to the windows. In the street an altercation was taking place between two drivers. "You come here with these fringe problems," he said. "Why can't you admit to yourself that our beliefs tempt you, why don't you enrol in one of our classes?"

Balthasar shook his head. "You misunderstand. Your anthropomorphic god, Heaven with Mary in the flesh—how could that tempt anyone, unless you had a very weak mind? Or," he added with a bright smile, "unless you were Dante?"

Martinez stood up. "In that case—"

"I'm not being sarcastic, Father Martinez. My questions deal with historical logic within history."

Martinez sighed. "Anyway—"

"One more thing. Please. I have a seal, a coat of arms of someone. At the library today someone looked at it for me with a

125

quartz lamp. This is what it says, I wrote it down, 'Exurbe Domine et judica causam tuam.' Can you place that for me?"

" 'Exsurge Domine et judica causam tuam.' I think the Vulgate has Deus, not Domine. It's from Psalms, somewhere in the middle. 'Rise, Lord, and judge Your cause.' Or, 'and argue Your cause'."

"Wow. And it means?"

"It means what it says."

"But I mean, does it refer to something special?"

Martinez sighed. "Is it important to you? I'm asking because I am a very busy man. Is it more than that logic within logic or whatever you just told me?"

"It is important."

"All right, I'll look it up for you. I'll call you. Or call me. Not tomorrow, please."

It took Balthasar three days to get hold of Father Martinez; his calls kept being answered by an uncommunicative housekeeper. And when the priest finally came to the phone, he sounded frigid. "You're not wasting my time with some silly game, are you, Balthasar?"

"No! Certainly not! What makes you think that?"

"Because we seem to have returned to that same subject you plagued me with at your first visit."

"I don't know what you mean, Father Martinez. I swear—"

"Sh. No need to swear. I thought that you—All right then. 'Exsurge Domine et judica causam tuam' was the motto of the Inquisition. John? Are you there? The seal, or perhaps better the banner of the Inquisition had a cross, an olive branch and a sword, and those words around it. That's what you wanted to know, right?"

"Well—yes—thanks. Thanks a lot for your trouble."

XLVIII

Perhaps comfort was to be found in this: it wasn't nightmares then or paranoia. Outside his own mind a reality existed, in this year 1984, connected to the eradication by fire of heretical thought. Even if this reality did not go beyond the stationery used by an

126

ex-Spaniard, Julian Lucas. The continuing reality of the human condition. That medieval hope. And terror.

He went to see Lucas. The thought of calling first did not enter his head, and he did not remember afterward if he had walked or run or taken a bus or taxi. He was sure the man would be there, and when the door was opened to him, he entered without greetings or explanation. Afterward he would remember that Lucas had not seemed surprised by this strange behavior.

"How, why, are you using that symbol?" were Balthasar's first words. "What are you up to? Is that why Miguel died?"

"What? Are you talking about my Pentagon seal?" Lucas answered with a little conspiratorial smile.

"Oh damn! Are you crazy? I mean, demented?"

Lucas seemed uncertain for one moment. He stood up and opened a rolltop desk. "Here," he said, handing Balthasar a metal embossing stamp. "I'm making no secret of it. It's worn, I'm having a new one made. Others use it too."

"Others? Amparo for instance, who killed his daughter?"

Lucas made a face, shook his head without answering.

"Exsurge Domine, that's not the Pentagon. Why tell such bull-shit?"

The other man had regained his calm. "It very well could be. The sword, the cross, the olive branch—more suitable than that almost extinct bald eagle."

Balthasar looked around for a chair and sat down. Why did I come, he thought. I suddenly don't seem to know any more what this is for. Huelca? Miguel? Andrea? I must see this through now.

Lucas sat down opposite him, tapped him on his knee. "Take our Spain," he said. "It was in the winter of 1808 that Napoleon came to Spain. He immediately abolished the Inquisition. Do you imagine Spain has been a happier country since?"

"Are you mad? I guess if you are, you wouldn't know your-self."

"I'm as sane as a bell. Isn't that an expression? Very appropriate too, bells have warned us through the centuries, have warned us in the West against the invasions of the barbarians. Listen, John, calm yourself. Miguel was mugged by a junkie in Miami, that's a safe assumption. Okay, yes, it would have been better all around if he'd stayed away from New York. We respected his past, he was a man then whatever else he was, an *hombre*. We didn't know he had become a professional Red and had stayed a Red. We turned our backs on him. Nothing more. We are not in the business of bumping off old men."

"What business are you in?"

"The business of Truth. That's what my seal stands for."

"For God's sake. Please, Lucas. Do you really think you can have an argument at this late date about the merits of burning people at the stake? Do you think that's why I'm here, to argue that? And for that matter, why are you here? Why are you in this country, why don't you go back where you came from? That's an expression too. Go back to your barbaric Pamplona."

Lucas stared at him, got up again and rummaged in his desk, giving Balthasar the odd idea that he was going to show him a Certificate of Naturalization. Lucas came up with a pack of cigarets, however. "Spanish," he said. "Sometimes hard to get. But I've stuck with them, all those years. Have one." He put the pack down in front of Balthasar. "My friend," he then said, "Let me assure you that I am more in harmony with the current trends of thought in this country than you appear to be."

He produced his lighter as Balthasar had taken a cigaret from the pack, but Balthasar leaned back.

"Consider this," Lucas said. "It's so simple. No human tragedy is comparable to the fate we all share. The fate of vanishing. A man can never hope to reconcile individuality and eternity. We feel there is only one way to create peace and happiness on this earth and that is through certainty. With that we're saying, *orthodoxy*. Every heretic, no matter how 'well-meaning'—a pointless term—is an enemy of all men."

Balthasar remained silent, looked around the room, at the photographs from the Spanish civil war.

"I think you're beginning to see our point," Lucas added.

The Andalusian soldier falling backward between life and death. Beyond consolation. What if he had seen that camera point at him the instant the bullet hit him, wouldn't that have been the greater inhumanity? We have lost respect for our own state, for the human condition.

That is why I am here. Certain acts, certain cruelties, are not bearable. It is not conceivable that we still. . . .

"Are you?" Lucas urged. "Are you seeing it?"

"Yes, sure," Balthasar answered. In harmony with the current trends of thought in this country. The way to deal with this is to lean back, as in jiu-jitsu, to pretend, to pretend.

"The poster," Lucas said with a smile. "You were led to my poster, my friend. The moment of truth, the fight against the beast. On the twenty-second of June of the year 1941 we began the last auto-da-fé."

Balthasar's hands trembled. I can't go on with this. "Lucas, my friend," he said, trying to imitate Lucas's tone of voice, "whether I see your point or not, and no matter who those 'we' are you keep on about . . . What I mean to tell you is, you don't sound much like a Spanish officer to me and you don't sound like an American corporal either. More like some kind of crackpot home-grown philosopher. That stuff about orthodoxy is not as great as you seem to think, it's a *Reader's Digest* dog's dish from what Dostoievski wrote a hundred years ago. In fact, why don't you go fuck yourself."

He fled from the room and the apartment, the unlit Spanish cigaret still in his hand.

LXIX

It was raining outside. At the corner the wind from the Hudson blew up his raincoat and a sudden burst of rain drenched his knees. Dammit.

The seal under which people were burned to death.

I must try and understand what being burned to death means, what being tortured means. It is what sets mankind apart, not their thinking. Homo Sapiens, shit. Homo Torquens if that's Latin. Man the Torturer. A reality I refuse to coexist with, the idea of our bodies, these sad sacks of organs, going at each other. We have atomized mankind into a hundred species. Or into five billion species, each one alone. And that doesn't even tell it. No animal does it to another.

You sit in your cell. They appear with that horrendous yellow

129

robe with the flames on it. As if for a game played by insane children.

Why put it on? I will resist, tear it to shreds. Why did those men and women wear them and walk in procession as if they accepted the rules of this unnatural game?

For the greater good of the Church, like those Moscow confessions in the thirties for the greater good of the Party? But they must have seen that Church, their tormentor, as the enemy, as evil.

I will not act that way, I will not do anything to help give sense and order to this human chaos. Men will have to hold me down as they put the robe on me. They'll have to tie my hands while I spit in their faces. They'll be muttering prayers all the while, shivering when they touch my skin in an anticipatory sadism, appearing to them as godly fervor.

Off to the field of the auto-da-fé, the hot and dusty town square of Huelca. Pilgrims watching, tourists watching from hotel windows, yellow German tour buses, *Auto-da-fé Reise*.

I alone am being dragged or carried, embarrassing my fellow victims. Perhaps I am the only one who believes in death. Time turning more and more slowly and yet also faster and faster. The very last instances ever of moving my legs, the executioner trying to tie me to the pole. Do not stand still for this, do not accept it, fight him.

The timelessness while the executioner binds the other heretics, timelessness because it is only seconds and yet endless time, from the moment he drops his torch into the kindling until I feel the heat of the little flames. Then the total fear and the total pain filling me.

But pain remains a mystery to me. I do not grasp why we cannot turn it off, why we cannot refuse its signals.

He arrived home wet through and his teeth were chattering. He dropped his clothes on the bathroom floor and crept into bed. But he got up again and went to get the box of kitchen matches.

He sat up in bed, lit a match, and moved his left hand toward it. Warmth, finally pain. A small pain which showed its potency though, its inherent character of becoming huge.

He tried a second time. I am too cowardly to do this as it must be done. But why, why pain in my hand, since all emotions spring from my brain? Then, unintentionally, he had let the match burn down to his fingers. He felt real pain but held on, until he had to drop the match with a smothered cry. There is a secret here, fakirs know it, Apaches used to have it. We better all study it, and now. But he felt foolish. He held his burned fingers under the tap, put away the matches, and turned the hole which had been burned in the sheet.

When Diana got home he told her he had caught a cold. He was shivering and she put an extra blanket on the bed.

"Diana, I got a little book from England on my desk today, it's called *Gentleman's Recreation*. Seventeenth century sporting hints. You know the hint for training young bloodhounds? You catch a deer in a net, then you cut off its left forefoot and set it free, and have the hounds catch it."

"Stop it."

"You'll say, that was long ago. But the 1983 American deer hunters' manual had this, 'If the bullet goes through the animal, so much the better. It will leave a good blood trail to follow.' "

She shook her head.

"In a way it cheers me up," he said. "It makes me think, we deserve all that's coming to us."

He did wake up with a cold but when he phoned in sick, Oliver's secretary sounded so unresponsive that he decided he'd better get back to work in the afternoon. A letter, in English, was on his desk from Miguel's Barcelona publisher: "We think we will want to publish the work."

Well, will you or won't you? Think, schmink.

"Some problems have to be taken care of first." The final chapters appeared to be written too hastily, they said, and perhaps connected with that, they had had certain inquiries about the circumstances of Mr Ruiz's death.

Balthasar immediately set himself to answer. Surely they could take care of any editing the book might need? Any hastiness was caused not by the "circumstances" of poor Mr Ruiz's death but more likely by the fact that he had been living on a hundred dollars a month pension. Perhaps they should now draw up a contract and send some money to the man's daughter? Yours sincerely. Go fly a kite.

Now for the first time he had a look at the Xerox of Miguel's manuscript. He could translate bits and pieces here and there; it was very neat, a beautiful handwriting. He saw that Miguel had used the margins for personal notes and reminders, telling himself to check this or that name or date. "Thank John" it once said in English. And on one of the last pages he had written, "'Each and every one of us will pay on demand his share of the sacrifice. . . .' Use this in an answer to Lucas." It's a quote, I've seen it somewhere. Che Guevara? Maybe that made them nervous in Barcelona. If I'd seen it, I'd have x-ed it out.

His share of the sacrifice. Miguel, what did you mean with that? Why the hell didn't you tell me?'

"Kathleen, Aileen," Diana said. "Do you like them? I'd like a really Irish name for her, if it's a her. Kathleen is my mother's name. And Robert for a boy? Robert Emmet was a family hero of ours."

"But then there's also his or her Dutch-hero ancestor's name . . . Look at you, you're blushing. Did you think you'd done it all alone?" She is blushing; that's just what she does think.

"What was his name again?" she asked. "You mean the dominie, right?"

"Yes—don't worry, there's not much you can do with it. Unless you want the baby to be called Bekker as a first name. Or Balthasar Balthasar. I settle for an Irish hero. As long as it's rebellious, as long as it's an underdog name. Miguel once told me your mother was an underdog."

"Tomorrow I'm going to my first exercise class," she said. "I'm very late with it, I had to work myself up to it. It's at seven, in the Lexington Avenue Y. Will you come with me?"

As her time came nearer, Diana's sense of vulnerability had increased; she often worked at home or went in for the morning only, and she read items about street accidents or muggings with great trepidation.

"Will you come with me?" she asked again.

He had not listened; his thoughts had wandered. We are all underdogs, we did not inherit the earth.

"Come with you?" he asked, confused.

"Is that so crazy? Some of my friends' husbands—Anyway, come tomorrow."

"Yes, yes, of course," he said hastily, still not understanding. Wherever.

L

What was happening to Diana during these months? How could she be so little aware of the turmoil John Balthasar was in? She probably was aware of some of it without letting it reach her.

In Diana's world there was a wall between private lives and the deeds of public figures past or present. She did not really expect these to have a bearing on herself, let alone to possibly doom her.

Thus she misunderstood and feared John's ideas about the world. They showed a quality in him of being attracted to disaster. She had once probed Dr Helfrich on this and the analyst had spoken the words "death wish". Presumably he would help John conquer that; she did not know John was not seeing the man. Meanwhile, the less said, the better. She was superstitious about it; John's words and feelings could threaten her baby as much as if he carried a virus.

She had always been a very private woman although open with some of her friends and especially with the people she worked with. She had been much more free in her sex life than they, or certainly than Balthasar, knew. She had always been very discreet. More than that: it had not touched her all that much, it was experiment, part of modern life, she told herself, a sin of indulgence to be confessed just like gluttony. For she was a sensual woman and had used men more than they might have used her. She had married poor Hubert because she disliked the idea of promiscuity once she separated it from the intense excitement of having her body invaded. Hubert had been meant to satisfy her body and allow her to be left alone by it.

She liked John's physical presence, he was manly and yet (and there was surely a "yet" here in her experience) serious, a seriousness her mother had confirmed for her, for her mother's standards were high and John was the first friend of Diana's she had not been ironic about afterward. Diana wanted a baby; she thought he'd be a good father. She meant he'd have good genes to pass on. She didn't

133

mean that he would be a good family man; she had never thought
that far.

She did not see her life in terms of love. From her mother she had
inherited a hard-boiled practicality about the ramifications of family
life. Balthasar would fall in line with that. She thought that deep
down he was more serious about religion than she was herself.

She was apprehensive about all kinds of private calamities but she
was basically at peace. The people in her office were sympathetic
and interested in her "condition" as they all called it. They brought
her pillows for her chair and insisted she drink milk in the coffee
break. She no longer disliked anything about her job.

She was happy.

It is no great secret that people may live in complete intimacy and
have no idea what goes on in each other's heads. A string of
circumstances and happenstance had worked on keeping Balthasar's thoughts hidden from her. As for him, he did not try to
share them; he too would have looked at that as exposing her to a
kind of infection. He was fighting them because he was becoming
more and more afraid of their irrationality.

She neither helped him nor steeled herself against any shocks to
come.

LI

Then a letter arrived from Julian Lucas.

Nothing in it about their argument. Once, he wrote, Balthasar
had needed to see Amparo for his own peace of mind and the man
had agreed; now Amparo was in New York and needed to see him.
Would he come to Lucas's apartment next Monday at six o'clock?
They counted on him.

Balthasar discovered that he welcomed the idea. It had been a
mistake not to hear Lucas out; it could be a fatal mistake not to take
him seriously and to forget all about him. There was a potentiality of
evil there. Balthasar took various tranquillizers now and when he
woke up he did not remember his dreams, but had the feeling of
having been a subconscious spectator of evil. Nothing less than that.

Thus he went once more to Lucas's apartment. It was overheated although spring was in the air. Lucas was alone. "He's late," he said. "Amparo always keeps me waiting."

Balthasar sat down without speaking.

"Before you ran out of here that afternoon," Lucas went on, "my last Spanish cigaret in your hand, but that only by the way, I was trying to show you how orthodoxy is the key."

Despite his decision to string Lucas along, Balthasar kept silent.

It didn't appear to discourage Lucas. " 'All right,' you'll say, 'All right for orthodoxy. But which one? Why not for instance Marxist orthodoxy?' Ha! The answer is simple. We need a metaphysical orthodoxy. What can't be proved on earth, can't be disproved on earth. That's precisely the strength of that Russian, Solzhenitsyn. Without that, my friend, we are, in Dante's words, lost in this world."

Balthasar stood up, hung his raincoat over the back of his chair, and sat down again.

Lucas nodded. "A college graduate is too proud to answer a crackpot philosopher."

"I didn't leave with your last cigaret," Balthasar said. "There was a full pack and you insisted I take the damn thing. I don't even smoke. If you want me to stay here, you must cut out that kind of crap. And furthermore, Dante never wrote the words, 'lost in this world.' "

"Okay so you don't smoke. Okay so you know all those thousands of verses by heart."

The door opened and Amparo entered. Either Lucas kept the front door open, Balthasar thought, or the faithful all had keys. "I don't have to know them by heart," he answered Lucas, "Dante could not have written that because in his whole universe no one was lost."

It was Amparo and not Lucas who listened to his answer, Amparo with a frown of concentration on his face. "La Vida Nuova," he said.

"Vita," Lucas said angrily. "Vida is Spanish."

Amparo elaborately stripped himself of a trenchcoat. Under it he was wearing the camouflage jacket of the previous occasions, but this time with a webbed belt and a police revolver. He hung his coat and belt on a nail which was also holding up a very ugly tapestry showing Mary ascending to heaven. Then he turned and shook hands with Lucas. For Balthasar he had what he must have meant to be a humorous bow. "Your Spanish passenger again," he said.

Lucas poured glasses of rum. Balthasar refused his but the sweetish smell reached out at him through the dry, hot air of the room. He closed his eyes to master a rising nausea.

"Yes, the boot's on the other foot." This from Amparo. "Not so long ago, John Balthasar, you needed me to put your conscience at ease. Now it's my turn. Strange? I don't like you to think bad of me. Why not?" He looked toward Lucas and gave him a kind of wink but Lucas didn't react. "Because you may become one of us. Who knows. You told Lucas I had and I quote, I had killed my daughter. Why did you say such a terrible thing? Don't you think a Spanish father loves his daughter? How do you know that she *wanted* to be rescued? That she wasn't ashamed to face her father?"

"Ashamed?" Balthasar asked, turning pale. "Amparo, or Captain Willers, or Sergio, or whatever you want to be called—today it must be pretty damn clear to you that you were responsible for her fate. I don't know what happened with you in the Maya police station, I don't want to know. But she stood up for you, didn't she. You talk about shame when a girl is forced to take to the street, but you don't talk about shame when her father changes sides? When he becomes buddies with the men who tortured his daughter, who staged—" He was about to speak of the Huelca auto-da-fé but didn't. They mustn't think I'm their enemy. But right now I can't keep this up. He got to his feet and grabbed his coat.

"Wait," Amparo said.

The man had changed again, Balthasar thought, only now properly focusing on him. He was fatter still but also softer, and he spoke and moved in a curiously jerky way. He reminds me of a mongoloid child.

"Where do you get your information about my daughter?" Amparo asked. "And how do *you* fit in with all this display of emotion? You met the girl for ten minutes, ten years ago. What is all this to you? She is *my* daughter."

Balthasar looked from one to the other. What is there safe to say to them.

136

"Pay attention, Gabriel," Lucas said to Amparo. "This man here just now called you Sergio. He's in the know, this one. He knows much more than you realize."

A silence in which Balthasar heard faraway cries, a woman's cries perhaps. I won't deny her again. To his own amazement, he spoke the words, "I loved Andrea."

The two men stared at him. Again, he fled from that apartment.

LII

When he got back to West 68th Street, he found Diana waiting for him in the lobby. "I'll be late!" she cried. "Where were you?"

"Late for what?"

"Oh for God's sake, John. You promised to come to my childbirth class with me. You look just terrible."

They had to take a taxi now. "Do you need me all the same?" he asked.

"There are all those long corridors there with strange characters hopping about. I guess I'm a coward."

"I'm sure you're supposed to feel that way. Nature protecting your baby. I'd be scared too of hopping characters. Maybe they have a hopping class."

She wasn't paying attention to him but looking nervously at the traffic. "You know that many girls have their husbands with them right through, in the delivery room?"

"Would you like that? I'll do it if you want me to."

"I don't know yet."

I hope I'd have the guts, he thought. How strange to make love to a woman once you've seen her like that. No mystery any more to her belly. But no, a different kind, a mystery of tenderness.

The softness of life. How lucky people have been all those centuries with children their guarantees for the continuation of life. Instead of hostages. Eventually, I by myself wouldn't give a good goddamn any more if they blow up our world or let it die under its curtain of ashes as they now say. Maybe. Maybe I wouldn't. But with this baby, I'll be thinking, just let him get to be ten, or then, fifteen, twenty-one. . . .

They were sitting on pillows on the floor of the gym, there was much laughter and jokes. He heard Diana introduce him and he half stood up and smiled at everyone.

His hand found a sheet of paper in his pocket and he couldn't think what it was. He pulled it out. Of course, the Lucas letter asking him to come and see Amparo. He was told to get hold of Diana's heel and to pinch when the command was given. He put the letter back in his pocket and tore it to bits with his left hand, while holding on to Diana's foot.

"Pant—pant—pant—pinch and blow," the instructress called out. She was a young woman with long dark hair. A nice face. An aloof face.

Diana had taken off the low-heeled shoes she was wearing and put them beside her pillow. He noticed they were badly scuffed at the back—beneath Diana's aloofness, such vulnerability had been waiting. He turned to her, but her eyes were closed, her face serene.

Pant-pant-pant-pinch and blow.

How sane this place is, how beautifully sane.

LIII

There had been a sign on a notice board at St Joseph's, the church where they were married, "Confessions—Saturdays 4 p.m." He went there.

The church appeared empty. He wandered up the aisle, not knowing how to go about this. Someone pulled at his sleeve. Two old ladies were sitting there, next to each other, dressed in black both. Submerged in the dim light. The one who had stopped him pointed at a little red lamp over a door beside the altar. He nodded and sat down too.

It became a long wait. The ladies took their time. Repeatedly he decided to leave. He knew before setting out that this was an unreasoned enterprise; even so he felt it was something he must try, or rather, have tried. He wasn't certain about what he was going to say.

Now he was alone waiting in the dark hall. The green light above the door went on. The second woman shuffled out without looking at him.

He opened the door to a cubicle without a chair; a wooden step became visible and he kneeled on it. Through a wooden screen he saw a light shining on the priest, a young man. The priest turned off this light.

"Bless me, Father, for I have sinned," Balthasar said, the peculiar statement which Diana had assured him was custom.

The priest asked him when he had last been to confession. He had a pleasant voice, an Irish accent.

"Oh, a long time, a very long time," Balthasar muttered.

There was a pause. "Yes, my son?" the priest said.

Balthasar took a deep breath. He tried to shift his position; the wood hurt his knees badly. He could feel his heart beat very fast. Let me think sharply now.

"This confession is to a responsibility," he said. "The responsibility for death through fire."

He heard something like a cough or gulp from behind the screen. Yes Father, I have something different for you from gossip or jealousy of the neighbors.

"Whose death?" the priest asked in a hoarse voice.

"Many. Many deaths. Slow deaths, of men and women burned alive."

The priest cleared his throat again. "You have come here with a clear head and in full command of your senses?"

"Yes, Father."

"Very well. Continue."

"That is all I have to say. What I must know is this, is there forgiveness for such a crime?"

Another pause, then the priest said slowly, "We are taught that to God no crime is too great to be forgiven, if there is true contrition, and penance."

"No crime is too great to be absolved by you?"

"The Church knows reserved sins, so-called." The priest's voice was wary now. "Those I cannot absolve, they must be heard by the Bishop. However, that is for later." He seemed to hesitate and then asked, "My son, are you an arsonist?"

Balthasar almost smiled in the dark. The pain in his knees

had become hard to bear; he half stood up, then kneeled again.

"No," he answered. And then he said, "I am not speaking for myself."

"You cannot confess to the sin of another man. We are taught that confession must be auricular and private."

"The high priest confesses to the sins of others on the Jewish Day of Atonement."

"Did you come here now in a spirit of seriousness?" the priest asked. He sounded relieved, and very Irish.

"I did."

"Well then. You're not a high priest, are you, and we're not Jewish. You talk of a terrible crime. If you really know about such a crime, you must try and have its author come to me himself. But I can't discuss this any further here, this is not the place. Do you understand what I told you?"

"I was not speaking of arson," Balthasar said. "I was speaking of execution through fire. And the author of this is you yourself, your church. I am asking you to absolve your own church."

He could hear the priest catch his breath. The man seemed about to speak but did not; a door opened and closed; the priest had left the confessional.

Balthasar felt himself redden. It was as if he was suddenly coming to his senses. What am I doing, he thought. He got up with difficulty and looked around the door. He saw no one. He well-nigh ran out of the church and breathed a slow sigh of relief when he had turned the corner.

It was the end of a lovely spring day. The light, after the gloom inside, was dazzling.

LIV

That feeling of relief stayed with him on his bus ride uptown. As he got off at his stop, he saw Diana come out of a store and walk toward their building; he hurried to catch up with her.

"Do you know this is the first time ever we've met in the street, you and I?" he asked.

"But we're half a block from home, it's less than a miracle."

140

"Never mind, it's nice, it means getting the better of this town. Let's not go in yet, let's go sit on that new terrace around the corner."

She hesitated.

"Come on, it's a rare evening, not too cold and not too hot."

"All right then, if we sit back from the traffic. I can't sit in the car fumes."

She ordered orange juice for herself. "I know I'm a terrible drag," she suddenly announced. "I don't recognize myself."

"Well, it's a long haul."

She looked around her, at the people at other tables, the passers-by, two cab drivers talking to each other at the light until a car behind them started to honk. "It isn't even that. I'm in good shape. It's the idea that this city is so threatening, it's threatening the poor thing. I don't feel safe. Maybe in my office, and at home in my bedroom. I know it's crazy."

Your baby is threatened. We are threatened. "It's okay," he said, "It'll all be okay. It'll all come out in the wash."

She smiled now. "That dates you, that expression."

"I don't mind. I am a wise old man."

"Yes, it will be all right, won't it?" she asked.

"Absolutely."

"But it hasn't been fair to you. You thought you were marrying a fashionable chick, didn't you?"

"Guess where I came from just now. Confession."

"John. No kidding. Are you coming over to us? But what did they say? And what did you confess, heh?"

"That's a secret, isn't it, between me and the priest."

"I was just joking."

"I know. I'll tell you some day. It wasn't what you think. But the point is, I can see how it makes you feel nice. I know there's no reality to it, I think there isn't, I mean God doesn't enter into it, but it makes you feel good. Just as something between two people. Even in my case."

"Why 'even'? Didn't he give you absolution?"

"I didn't ask for it, not like that."

"Oh. . . ." She was puzzled. "Where did you go? Shall I tell mother? She'd be pleased."

141

"Well, she may get the wrong idea—I went to our wedding church in the Village. I remembered their sign. Not the same priest, a young Irishman. Are you cold? Shall we go home now?"

"No, I'm okay, it's nice here, I'm glad you made us do this. John—you're okay now, aren't you? You're not brooding too much about Miguel's death any more, and all that stuff, are you?"

"No, I'm okay."

"You still have nightmares, don't you?"

"No, not really. I take my pills."

"Sometimes when I'm awake, I hear you moan and groan."

"Oh God really? Just give me a kick. Honestly. Do. You know what's so pleasing about this confession business, it's so old-fashioned. Like house calls. Isn't it odd they are doing it still? And for free? I bet you they'll switch to tapes soon, or some kind of video hook-up." As he spoke, he realized that the sensation of a burden having been lifted, had gone. Those hours in St Joseph's Church were becoming blurred; soon they'd sink away.

"When this is over," he said, "when the baby is born, perhaps we should go away, not vacation I mean, just go, to some place I don't know where."

"We'd have a hard time finding another apartment."

"Yes, that's true of course."

She had a little smile, and took hold of his hand. "I know that's not what you meant. You must find your peace right here, you know, with me. With us. Here, feel." And she put his hand on her belly.

LV

Monday morning brought the expected talk with Mr Oliver. The man was friendlier than John had thought but there was a disconcerting aspect to this friendliness: "We know you're under stress," he told Balthasar. "We can see how your work would suffer from that."

"Well, no, not really. How is that supposed to show? What have I done wrong?"

Oliver shuffled the papers on his desk and glanced in a folder. "Nothing wrong, nothing really wrong. Your colleagues simply feel you're somewhat disturbed."

"Oh. Well, I'm not, not in the way you mean it. Of course, with my salary, and New York rents. . . ."

"There's a counselor available for our staff," Oliver said. "Not a psychiatrist, simply a man or perhaps it's a woman, I'm not sure now, who is trained to help people with their personal problems. Why don't you make an appointment through personnel, take it from there?"

"Well, if you insist."

Oliver started to smile. "You know, John, don't you, you're the only person on your level without a library degree? It's a good thing I wasn't here at the time, you would never have been hired." His smile broadened into a laugh. "You sneaked through, didn't you? And your contract, I had a look at that, it isn't standard at all."

"You mean I'm out?"

"No, no, don't jump to conclusions. You've done a lot of good work. Let's take it one at a time, let's see what the counselor thinks."

"Is that it then, Gene?"

"That's it, John. By the way, did you ever trace that Dante?"

"Excuse me?"

"That nineteenth-century Dante that the binders lost."

"Oh, that one. They're still looking."

And fuck you, Gene Oliver. Sneaked through. Disturbed. Maybe you should be a bit disturbed.

His telephone rang. I won't answer that. Let's think this through first. How I would love to quit. But that's out of the question, obviously. The baby. That damn apartment. But I am assuredly not having myself probed by any counselors either.

The telephone started ringing again. He picked it up, it was Lucas.

"Shit," Balthasar muttered.

"Shit? Why shit, my friend?"

"Sorry, nothing."

"Meet me for lunch, we must talk. The Toledo, West 35th Street. In half an hour?" Lucas asked.

"No, no, impossible. I can't get away. What is it?"

"I will come to you then in half an hour. Okay?"

"Eh—well, okay. Not in my office, I'll meet you in the North Gallery. Third Floor, through room 315."

When he walked in, he immediately saw Lucas, at the far end of the first table with a pile of books in front of him. Balthasar sat down across from him and Lucas put his hand on his hand. "My friend—"

Balthasar pulled his hand away. That's all I need, when Oliver is told I had a rendezvous with some man in the reference room. "I only have ten minutes," he said.

Lucas shook his head. "You keep turning up and escaping, you are tempted to join us and are afraid to do so at the same time, isn't that true?"

A pause. "Yes," Balthasar answered. "Yes, perhaps so."

"It is a fearful temptation, John, but I tell you, resist it, don't join the victims! You've been to Huelca, you were led there, you have seen and thought about our poster. You recognized our seal immediately."

"But who are *us*? What does that poster mean?"

"I am sure you understand quite well. Have the courage to understand!"

"For Chrissakes, keep your voice down, Lucas, this is a public library. You want to get me fired?"

The excitement in Lucas's face vanished. He looked around; Balthasar thought he might walk out. But then he said, in an exaggerated whisper, "The final auto-da-fé, gone underground in the year 1945, is destined to reappear. We, who lit the flames for the first auto-da-fé in the Americas, in Mexico, in 1574, will be alive to extinguish the flames of the last one!" His voice was rising again.

Balthasar had the sudden comforting certainty that Lucas was insane. "What is all this, it sounds like the Olympics, what do you want from me?" he asked.

"I want you in because you're an artist like me. You will counter-balance Amparo who is a military man only, who thinks

144

with his guts. You are a believer, are you not? Do you want Moscow to become the Third Jerusalem? A Red Jerusalem? Rome, almost as Red? Jerusalem, under the Jews? Madrid will be the Third Jerusalem, my friend, the true daughter of the Church, on the ashes of—" He peered at Balthasar.

"The ashes of—?"

Lucas produced a kind of cramped smile. "I'm speaking in metaphors of course," he said. "Reflect on it."

"Could you folks keep your voices down, for God's sake?" a man behind Balthasar said.

He turned around. "I'm sorry, I'm just leaving."

He stood up and so did Lucas. "Reflect on it," Lucas repeated and hurried out of the room without waiting for Balthasar.

LVI

Balthasar went back to his office and sat still at his desk for a time. Then he started rummaging through his drawers, looking for the calling card which the white-haired FBI-man had given him during the interview about Miguel's death. That now seemed a very long while ago. He couldn't find it and ended up turning his desk drawers over on to the floor. There it was.

He telephoned the FBI and was told the agent in question was no longer posted in New York. If it wasn't a personal call, they'd pass him on to someone else in that department.

Not that young man for Chrissakes. No, a soft, deep voice, a black guy presumably. Mr Harris. Yes, Mr Harris could come and see him in the library. At four that afternoon.

"We were glad about your call," Harris told him. "You have some new idea about the death of Mr Ruiz?" He looked in a folder while he was talking. They all do that.

"Correct me if I'm wrong," Balthasar answered, "but I had the impression at the time that you were, eh, looking for a Cuban connection?" Harris showed no reaction to this and Balthasar went on, "Ruiz was in touch with Spaniards here, or better Spanish-born Americans, exiles from one side or the other in their civil war. There are strange characters among them. Did you ever look into that angle?"

"I'm not too familiar with the state of our investigation at this point. Suppose you simply give me your view, sir."

Balthasar closed his eyes for a moment. I don't feel very clear-headed. I didn't eat today. Am I handling this right? Why are my thoughts crowding me so? I didn't used to be like this.

"Okay," he said. "There is a Julian Lucas, of a thousand and something Riverside Drive, I can look it up. His friend Gabriel Amparo who seems to be training mercenaries in Southern Florida, a place called Paolita. Also known as Captain Willers. Lucas was here earlier today. He rambles, maybe he's not all there. Either way, he's a religious and a political fanatic. He uses, if you please, the seal of the Spanish Inquisition on his letters. He talks about the new Third Jerusalem, and that would be Madrid, to be built on the ashes of the former Third Jerusalem. You see, Moscow used to be called the Third Jerusalem."

He thought Harris's attention was wandering but the man now blinked and then said, "Did it? I thought that was Kiev."

"What?" Balthasar hesitated. "However that may be, Mr Harris, I don't relish the role of a police informer. But Miguel, Mr Ruiz, was killed. There's a connection. Miguel was a radical, a Basque, a bitter opponent of the Franco government. Those two men and their buddies, I don't know how many they are, they're dangerous guys. I think they had Miguel killed. Why? I don't know. But Miguel had stuck to his civil war beliefs and those men were turncoats. Perhaps it was a revenge. Perhaps it was to shut him up. About Paolita, I mean."

Harris waited and when Balthasar remained silent, he asked, "And that is all you know about this, sir?"

"Yes, Mr Harris."

"I'll take it up at the Bureau. We may want to talk to you again at some future time. And don't call yourself an informer, please. You've done your proper duty as a citizen."

"Eh, yes . . . Don't you want Lucas's address?"

"We can find it." Harris was putting his coat on. I haven't impressed this man, Balthasar thought. He went on, "But all this goes beyond personal battles, that's the crucial thing, I think

nothing would please these men better than another World War."
As he spoke, he saw that Harris was concentrating on the locks of
his attaché case.

"We deal with any number of strange birds, Mr Balthasar. Don't
worry, the Bureau will know how to handle this."

I think he includes me among the strange birds, Balthasar
thought, watching Harris making his exit. Maybe he figured I was
making it all up. They're spooky guys, they don't react.

He walked over to the Reading Room and looked up *Auto-da-fé*
once more in the encyclopedias. It was as Lucas had said: the first
one on American soil had been staged by the Spaniards in Mexico.
The year had been 1574, and they had burned two converted
Spanish Jews, one Moor, and a large but unspecified number of
baptized but lapsed Indians, those last ones "with slow fire". The
text explained that meant the executioner had used green wood.

LVII

Well, I've done what I could, he thought. To begin with I've
invoked the heavenly powers and after that the worldly powers, ha
ha.

The first few days after the visit of agent Harris, Balthasar kept
himself on a kind of alert when the phone rang or when he left the
library at night: he assumed that Lucas might be lying in wait for
him, to call him a Judas and who knows, to try and knife him. But
nothing happened.

He telephoned the personnel counselor (a man, whose name he
didn't catch). That was as far as he'd go to meet Oliver's request.

The counselor asked him what he expected of the service and
Balthasar answered that it hadn't been his idea but that of his
boss.

"But it's not something you would go through just to please your
boss?"

"Oliver, that's the boss, tells me I'm under stress. I'm sure he's
right. But we all are. Or should be, shouldn't we? Everything has
changed. When I read Dante . . . or Proust, those cups of tea,
beauty of church steeples, or, Christ, just any old whodunit, you

think what the hell is all the fuss about. We have cyanide for our last sacrament, did you read about those Brown students?"

"Eh, no. What was that about?"

"Oh never mind."

There was a silence at the other end, then the counselor, not any less cheerful, "Mr Balthasar? John? Are you there? We should talk about these things eye to eye. Don't you agree that would be better? I'm at the walk-in clinic in Bellevue, every weekday from four to six except Wednesdays."

"Bellevue?"

"Don't let that name put you off. We treat everything from flat feet to, to a penchant for alcohol."

"And what are you going to treat me for?"

The counselor ignored that question. "Unfortunately, I won't be available for the next two weeks. Can we make it for the week after?"

"I guess so. I'll call."

"In the meanwhile, remember, John, mankind has always gone through violent times. There've always been wars and cataclysms, and we're still here, aren't we? The important thing is for each of us to realize our own potential."

He accompanied Diana to her exercise class. He hadn't told her about any of this, either about Lucas or about the FBI. They took the crosstown bus through the park and started walking down Lexington Avenue.

"You sure you're okay?" she asked.

"Sure. Sure sure. It's starting to rain."

"Oh, it's only a couple more blocks. You know, you must help me think of a present for mother."

"Right. Eh, I forgot why."

"Oh come on now, I told you about it yesterday." She looked at his face and saw he didn't know. "You're supposed to be married ten years or so before you stop listening when your wife talks to you. Mother is going to this congress in Chicago, and then on to friends in Michigan for a couple of weeks. She'll be away on her birthday."

"Oh, yes."

"Don't look put off, she'll be back in plenty of time for the baby.

148

She's coming through here first, she'll take her present with her and open it on her birthday. We're very sentimental about these occasions. It has to be something nice, and small."

"I want to give her something too," he said. "I've got something nice and small. Does she read Italian?"

"Italian? No, why would she?"

"Just an idea. A silly idea. Never mind."

It was soothing to sit on the gym floor and listen to the conversations, about buying a pram, about being stuck in Bloomingdale's basement when you had to find a toilet to pee. Breathing exercises and a break with orange juice and cookies.

Not a word about the world at large and its deathly politics. He said something about that to Diana. She shrugged and smiled. "But of course. All we care about is having a baby."

"Lucky."

"You should do the same. Come on, John, it's our baby. Try. Try!"

He nodded vehemently. Of a sudden he felt different, light. Jesus, why not. I've done what I could. What I can. It'll be all right now, and if it isn't, maybe we'll never know. I'll set my lights by this sane world here. "It's a deal," he said. "Now give me your heel to pinch."

LVIII

Afternoon. He felt quiet, working on a routine job of numbering the pages in an old manuscript. When his phone rang, he picked it up without stopping his work.

"Balthasar? Amparo here. I hear you've been busy."

Oh Jesus. He put the phone down on his desk, walked to the window, aware of Susan's eyes on him. He looked at the sky, went back to his desk.

"Hello, Amparo? Sorry, I can't talk to you." He hung up.

He grabbed his raincoat and went over to Susan. "Sue, sorry, something very urgent. If my phone goes, please tell them I had to go out. Out of town."

The following morning he was in early, before her, and he

approached his desk with circumspection, sure of finding various messages of Amparo's fury. But there weren't any, and there were no more calls from him.

When he came home on Friday of that week, Diana met him at the front door and told him in a whisper, "An old friend of yours is here waiting for you. Sergio something? I didn't catch the last name. Is it all right? He said he was on his way to Florida. I called the library but you'd already left."

"Sure, he's okay." He smiled reassuringly at her. His fear had vanished, I've been a coward, let him, let him try whatever he wants. The thing is to get him out of here first. "Don't worry," he told her, "I'll get rid of him, give me half an hour. Why don't I take him to a bar or something."

"Hello, Sergio." He held out his hand. Amparo, rather than pulling out any guns, shook it. Luckily the man was in a shirt and jacket this time. "Let's go have a drink somewhere, somewhere undisturbed. There's a nice bar around the corner."

He waited and swallowed. "Fine, sure," Amparo answered. "Good night, Mrs Balthasar. Thanks for the coffee."

They rode down in the elevator without a word. On Broadway, Amparo said, "No, let's go there." He chose a shabby little bar.

They sat down in a booth.

"Okay," Amparo said. "Okay. First, I am here to help you. But you've got to trust me. I have nothing to do with the death of Señor Ruiz. Can you get that through your head?"

Balthasar nodded.

"Now you could have done us a lot of harm, and it's no thanks to you that you didn't. But I blame myself too, I should have put you in the know."

He ordered two bottles of beer.

"Okay, that's first. Forget Ruiz. Second, appearances fool people. I look like a fat slob who doesn't know his ass from a hole in the ground, don't say I don't—" he waited one moment—"but that's Rosa's cooking. There are good lays and good cooks but she has it all. I'm the fat slob and Lucas in his white tee shirts and his ironed safari jackets is the cool thinker, right? Wrong. For your info, Lucas is senile if you ask me, he's some kind of reborn fanatic. That's to say, he's all right for what we need him for, but we have to

150

put it in his terms you see, he likes that stuff about Third Jerusalems and of course the bullfight poster which was his idea is a terrific vote getter—"

"Vote getter?" Balthasar couldn't resist asking. Shit. Just shut up and let him unwind himself, he isn't going to do any shooting, and get out.

"Means-of-propaganda. I knew he had queered you as soon as he reported that conversation to me. I could just figure it, him scream-ing about the Lord and you trying to damp it down, right, to keep your boss from hearing all that stuff."

Balthasar managed a smile.

"But, mi amigo. Never mind the Jerusalems. This is serious, this is for real. I trust you, you know I always have. And I know you loved Andrea, I believe you there. How, where, I don't even want to know."

"I—"

"Never mind that. It's why I'm here and why it didn't feel right to go back to Paolita without seeing you and without helping you. Not that I'd spell out those reasons to that very nice lady you have waiting for you around the corner—" He pointed with his thumb to the wall behind him. "I'm just kidding, John, just kidding, that's a lovely set-up you got there and you gotta protect it." He stopped to catch his breath and emptied his glass. "Well, protect it—This city, the Big Apple and all that shit, one day it's going to be flattened all the same, isn't it?"

Balthasar stared at him. Once more Amparo completely changed his manner. No more grinning, blinking or leering. He was quiet and seemed very subdued.

"I need some more beer," he said. "What about you."

LIX

The waitress brought beers, wiped the table. Amparo watched her patiently.

"We still speak from habit, don't we," he said, nodding his head, "about food and dames and all the rest of it, but we know. Those of us who do the thinking know that the balloon will go up one of these days, as the English say. Okay. No matter what they tell you, even then some of us will be all right, well, all right, we'll be forewarned, forearmed. Not fair? Sure, but that's always been the way of the world. Our people will be forewarned, and I'm including you for Andrea's sake, we'll have a chance. At least we won't get it in the middle of a traffic jam on the George Washington Bridge. What do we deliver in return? You know what my men in Paolita are for."

Balthasar swallowed. "No, I don't," he managed to say in his normal voice.

"You saw the tip of the iceberg. We got thousands of men. At least two thousand. Enough. They're catalysts, you know what that is. They are there to start the ball rolling where and when it suits us, not the other guys. Here, in Latin America, home base, with the odds all on our side."

He scrutinized Balthasar's face. "I know, it sounds rough, even when you had drawn your own conclusions." He shook his head. "It's simply being a case of choosing the tough option. Be the first on the draw after that, and with the sun behind you. A lot of my men are Spaniards, you'll be surprised to hear, they're the second and third generation Franco kids. You see how Spain is still important, not hardware-wise of course, but Spain is the only country that fought the Russkis and wasn't defeated. You aware of that? You know about the Blue Division and all that? These kids buy the idea that the Caudillo wanted it all this way, lying low when he had to but still get Spain in on the war. Win the war."

"The war?"

"World War Two. It was never properly finished, was it. Hitler started that on June the 22nd 1941, that's what Lucas is babbling about, a bullfight Sunday, would you believe it. But Hitler muffed it. There's no end to that war till we get the Russkis. Now you see. Lucas is no political man and there are millions like him, they need to see this in religious terms. It's too frightening otherwise. Here's the last generation of heretics and we have to send them to the devil. Missiles is the long-distance way of putting them at the stake. Credit Lucas for seeing it that way and putting it that way. It's a good against evil world, that's the message. There's a word for that. Manichean."

He waited for a reaction or a question.

"I know," Balthasar murmured.

"You see, I've done my homework too even if you won't hear me preaching like Julian. Manichean. Those Manicheans were burned themselves, in France. Fires for half a century. Did you know that?"

John Balthasar now had become very still inside. I will quietly listen to this. I will play the role necessary. He may be only raving and he may not. I have seen the men with the automatic rifles. "I have believed in Franco," he answered. "I was too young to know what it was really about, but there was something clean about it. About their song, 'Face to the Sun'. That was a very tricky thing, when a lovely young girl, your daughter, asked me to smuggle an anti-Franco terrorist out of the country."

He smiled at Amparo, who had been the terrorist.

Amparo reached over and squeezed his hand. "I know, my friend. Why do you think I'm sitting here? You can help a bit but so can a hundred other guys. It's like this, my people get warned. I have cards, ten thousand cards were printed with that seal of Lucas, the Domine thing. That's our warning. I don't know how many I'll be allowed to send out."

He pulled a card out of his pocket and held it out; when Balthasar failed to take it, he put it on the table. "I'd like to send 'em all out, but the big shots say, if we warn too many, then you may as well forget it, you'll get the same panics and the same log jams. It's very far from being a guarantee, we're not underestimating the fireworks of the Russkis. But even if the worst comes to the worst, it gives you a chance to die like a man, a soldier, if you see what I mean."

"Jesus."

"Be realistic. I'm not telling you anything you didn't really know, am I? Except for the cards, the gimmicks. There's always something like that on the fringe. I'm not kidding myself, if it weren't us they want to use, there'd be some other angle they'd play. Still and all, us it is."

"Well, no, I didn't know." Balthasar had trouble speaking and grabbed his glass, pretending to clear his throat with the beer.

"There's no point in kidding ourselves, no point in acting like those German Jews under Hitler, 'it won't be so bad', that kind of stuff. We have to get it over with, there's no choice, right?"

Balthasar nodded. Forgive me for that.

153

"You'll have a job," Amparo went on. "No big deal. The big deal jobs are on the inside. I'm not kidding myself, we're auxiliaries. But you can deliver something in return. The library system, interloans or whatever you call it, I've thought about that, it may be of some use to us. More reliable than the US mails maybe."

"I think, I think it uses the mails."

"Oh well, whatever. I'll think of something."

"And just for that, or for Andrea—"

"It's for her, sure." And now that grin reappeared on Amparo's face. "There's of course also the little matter that you seem to have been around the course all by yourself already, Huelca and the rest of it. And then old Lucas had to get the wind up your ass about poor Señor Ruiz, send you to the cops—I feel neater having you on the inside. Now I'm off to Paolita. You wanna drive me to the airport?"

"I don't have a car."

"No kidding. Well okay then, I'm off. Here, to settle the tab. Don't worry, money is not our problem."

LX

After Amparo had gone, Balthasar sat motionless for a long time. The waitress came over and asked him a question but he did not hear her. Finally he picked up the card Amparo had left on the table.

Here then was the Lucas seal, now clearly visible if badly printed: two ovals with the quote from Psalms running between them. A cross planted in the ground, an unhumble aggressive cross of thick, knotted wood, built to restrain a heretic burning on it, on one side of it the olive branch, on the other the sword pointing upward. The banner of the Inquisition, ordering God to "rise" and judge. If only. Or possibly that was what would happen. Judgment on humanity. The card was wet with beer and shedding drops in his lap; he held it above the table and turned it over. He saw that some kind of cartoon was printed on the back, it showed a little man in a nightcap trying to start a car with an old-fashioned crank handle. Underneath the drawing it said, "For Cold Starts, VARA Batteries".

For God's sake. An ad, a "funny" ad. He stared at it, he turned it over and stared again. That seal of doom and on the other side an ad for a car battery; but all this was unreal then, those men were simply a bunch of freaks playing out some enormous sick joke. Or was this supposed to be a profound symbolic comment on our world? Or am I crazy and imagining it all, maybe it's in my mind only, maybe I came here alone, there's only one glass on the table? For God's sake. For God's sake.

He went to the men's room, left the card sticking in the mirror, dabbed his face with water.

Out on Broadway he turned west, and walked all the way to the river. He wanted to pull himself together before getting back to Diana.

The small black waves of the Hudson in the evening wind; the consolation of nature. But that, too, will be gone, he said to himself.

The lights along the Jersey shore shining through the dark blue haze. The pain of America at dusk. He repeated those words half-aloud, the pain of America at dusk, without really knowing what he meant with them.

LXI

On Monday morning he was at the library when its doors opened. He called the FBI office. Mr Harris wasn't in yet. Yes, when he'd come in, he'd call back. "It's not what he thinks, it's urgent," Balthasar told them.

He decided to wait till half past eleven. At eleven o'clock, he called and got Harris.

"There's nothing new, Mr Balthasar," Harris immediately said. "I will call you when there is."

For God's sake. "I'm not calling you about Ruiz, I'm calling you about something more important. In fact, literally, nothing could be more important. I want to come and see you. Now."

"Can you give me an idea what we're going to talk about?" Harris asked.

"War."

A silence. "All right, Mr Balthasar. I'll come and see you, though. At four again?"

*

155

This time Harris brought a case which he placed on Balthasar's desk with some care. He's taping me, Balthasar thought. Good. "I did not ask to see you about Ruiz," he said. "And not even about that camp in Florida. I quite realize you probably knew all about that, and I wouldn't be surprised if it's okay with you. But this is going way beyond that, it's going as far as you can go in this world, this is about nothing less than a conspiracy, or that's how it looks, in which these mercenaries will be used to set off an incident leading to war. To atomic war. A plan to have Russia atom bombed, burned away. Even if we go too."

Harris looked surprised but nothing more.

"Mr Harris, I am not a strange bird quote unquote. I am sane. My involvement with this goes back ten years, it started with a magazine assignment I had in 1973. I told you about that seal of the Inquisition. It is to be a warning signal. There is a conspiracy, a conspiracy."

Am I right with that word, where did I get that angle? Suppose Amparo and Lucas and the rest of them are working for the Pentagon? "We're auxiliaries," that's what he said—But that's too crazy. Not too wicked, nothing would surprise me, but too amateurish. They wouldn't have any need for a bunch of aging Spaniards and kids playing soldier. He related the bar conversation with Amparo, leaving out only Andrea. "I hope you'll be discreet," he said, "Amparo considers me an ally."

As at their first meeting, Harris remained silent for a while, and then asked that same question, "And that is all you know about this, sir?"

"Yes."

"I shan't be dealing with this just by myself," Harris said, getting up. "We will be in touch. Did that man actually use the words, 'atomic war with Russia'?"

Had he? "I'm not certain. It was clear enough. Either he's a psychopath, or that's what he was talking about. Or maybe both."

"Both?"

"A psychopath. And a conspirator."

When Harris had left, he saw that Susan had gone too. She had turned off the lights in her part of the room which now was unusually

156

dark: the library was on a saving-electricity kick. The sky beyond the window was black.

He had decided to read about Manicheanism. The volumes were already on his desk. He felt exhausted. He shifted his chair and put his feet on the chair Harris had pulled up.

What sick ideas. What sick times. Harris had looked as if he dealt regularly with plans to blow up a few hundred million people. Maybe he'll simply be sending some guys over with a straitjacket for me. Maybe he'd be right.

Then he read pages and pages about old ideas and old religions, beautiful ones eradicated and vanished. The historical facts quickly became blurred in his mind.

What stayed was an image of vast, dark, lost centuries, a perished world of men and women who must have felt in their time, as he had felt in his time, that their world could not perish without a trace.

Those fires of the autos-da-fé in all the southern towns of France, in which the last of them were burned. The Manicheans.

How mysterious that that fat man with his camouflage jacket and his fresh shrimp had come up with this. Did he realize he was talking about the world of the victims when he used that word?

My passenger. And perhaps then part of him is still that man who walked away in the snowstorm.

We learned about things like those burnings in high school. We were told about such things. But we believed it was the past. We believed we had since moved to a *higher* time.

Now, kids must think, we will follow into oblivion.

Diana's mother knows this already. She said, the only difference is that now the heretics are farther away.

My dream from the past and my dream from the future are now coming together. We start history with the simple fire of burning wood. Green wood. My dreams do have meaning, and Amparo did not tell me anything I did not know. "A large number of men and women were burned at Carcassonne," that's what it said in one of those books just now. That's that town with the walls I drove through, not far from Marseilles. "A large number of men and women were burned at New York." That will be not be written down or ever read.

*

157

A cleaning woman looked around the door, did not see him, and turned off the last lights.

"Hold it," he cried, getting up and stumbling in the dark toward the door.

LXII

On Wednesday he called Harris and did not get through to him. He was asked to leave a message. The man did not call back.

On Thursday he called once more and was told Mr Harris was out of town, and if he'd leave a number they would make sure he'd be called back on Monday.

On Friday he telephoned the FBI office and did not give his own name. This time he got Harris on the phone. Harris sounded calm and friendly; he was very busy and he would surely have called Balthasar on Monday. There was nothing to report yet.

"But what do you mean, very busy? Doesn't this have top priority?"

"Sir," Harris answered, "You've done your part, please do not worry about it any more. It has gone to Washington, I've made a full report, believe me, they know what they're doing."

"Yes, yes, I hear what you're saying but—will you call me on Monday and tell me what's been decided?"

"Absolutely."

He had the feeling there'd be some reassuring news that Monday and it made the weekend easier for him. He walked downtown with Diana to get her mother's present and noticed with surprise that the trees were already in heavy leaf. Spring had come and almost gone without penetrating the fog. "New York's at its best on days like this," he said.

"You've been in a terrible funk, John, are you climbing out of it?"

"Absolutely."

"You're a manic depressive, that's for sure."

"Oh that's just a Helfrich word for being up and down. I'm sure most of us are."

"Well, he's helping you, isn't he?"

158

Those pleading sea-blue eyes of hers, what a fine woman, girl really pregnant and all as she is. Too beautiful. He stood still on the avenue and gently put his arms around her. "Yes," he said, "and you do even more."

Monday arrived; he was so certain of the reassuring phone call that he never set foot out of his office for fear of missing it. But no call came. Several times he started dialing the FBI number but each time he dropped the receiver back.

At half past four his phone rang; he picked it up with a tired "Yeah?" and it was the man from the FBI. "I have to see you," Harris said. "When would be convenient?"

"Any time. Now!"

"Tomorrow at four then, at your office."

"Why not tomorrow morning?"

"Tomorrow morning would be difficult," Harris answered.

"Okay, okay. Tomorrow at four."

He put his phone down and he felt comforted. I'm not alone. People are not all crazy.

He had to get out now. "I'll go buy us some coffees," he called out to Susan. "All right?"

"No, I won't have any."

"Oh come on. I'll treat you to a piece of apple pie."

In the coffeeshop he was nervous and in a hurry to get back. He installed himself at his desk. To read Dante. He hadn't looked at those books for a while. A bitter association, vague and unexplained, had stopped him. That had gone now, and it was important to make up for the gap. He put his feet up. Coffee, dictionaries. Read once again from that beginning. Peace.

La diritta via era smarrita

Harris made his punctual appearance. The moment Balthasar saw him he thought, I have been fooling myself again. Nothing has changed.

This time the FBI man put his attaché case on the floor after taking out some papers. "Thank you for seeing me so promptly," he said.

"I wish you wouldn't be so damn polite, Mr Harris. It's too important, too grim for that, don't you see?"

Harris had been on the point of handing Balthasar the papers but checked his movement. "You must not expect anything out of the ordinary," he answered. "I have no new facts."

"You haven't? You yourself said you had to see me!"

"I need your signature on these. It's not much more than a formality."

Balthasar swept some of the things on his desk to the side and dropped the papers in the cleared space. A ballpoint rolled on to the floor and a stapler crashed down after it. Harris looked at him but Balthasar didn't pick them up. He read the top sheet of the document; the letters were dancing in front of his eyes and he blinked to clear his vision.

"But this is nothing, these are printed forms. What *is* this?"

"They comprise a commitment that you will not talk or write about the matters we discussed with anyone but us."

"Comprise? *Comprise?* What kind of English is that supposed to be? Why all this? Why should I sign this?"

"I'm following instructions from Washington, Mr Balthasar. I understand all this is now classified material."

"But fuckit, you got it from me. Am I to keep it from myself now? Why don't you have my head cut off then, that's the best way."

Harris had a little smile in answer to that. "As I said, it is a formality, a precaution if you wish. If you'd read on, you will find it doesn't refer to your experiences only, it covers anything connected with it, other matters which you don't know of. And which I don't know of either."

"And what happens if I refuse to sign?"

"Nothing, nothing happens. Of course, you'd exclude yourself from any future news I may have."

"Oh damn—" He picked the ballpoint off the floor and signed. I'll do what I want anyway. Fuck 'em.

"All three copies," Harris said.

"Presumably, you wouldn't bother with stuff like this if Dooms-day were around the corner?" Balthasar muttered.

Harris smiled a little smile again while collecting the forms; Balthasar was not sure he had heard the question. Harris locked his case and stood up.

160

"You're not walking out of here like this?" Balthasar asked in a sharp voice.

"But we've transacted our business."

"Transacted? Are you people mad? I've had more of a reaction, bigger waves, when my tax return was a hundred dollars off! Are you folks bombproof yourselves? What can you be thinking of? I've made a dozen calls to get you on the phone, I want to know what's going on. I have a right to know. Never mind the fucking pursuit of happiness, what about our right to live, our children's right to live. I haven't delegated that to anyone, to my knowledge. I want to know if these men, Amparo and the lot, if they're cranks, or if they're conspirators, or if they're working for the United States government."

"I can't answer any of those questions," Harris replied calmly.

"I insist!"

"Because I don't know the answers myself."

"I want to speak to your boss, to the man in charge," Balthasar said.

"I'm in charge of this case."

"And just now you said you didn't know what was going on."

"I'm in charge of the New York end. Washington took over."

"Who in Washington? What is his name?"

Harris sighed loudly. "Do you have security clearance, Mr Balthasar?"

"What? No! Why would I?"

"It's useless to continue this conversation," Harris answered and left.

"What happened to you?" Diana asked him.

"Nothing, nothing."

"You're not seeing him, as you promised, are you? Why not?"

"Seeing who?"

She did not answer.

"I'm sorry," he said. "I'm not seeing Helfrich because I'm seeing a counselor at the library instead. It's free and he's very nice. I'm sorry I didn't tell you. These things embarrass me, I guess."

"All right, all right, John."

LXIII

He remembers the peculiar, special warmth of days in southern France. The sharp smells in the air of sun on pine trees. Of fires. These smells and that warmth on his skin come to him before he sees anything.

He is in a squat tower then, looking out through iron bars at a sun-drenched green landscape; the tower is part of a city wall. But knowing he is again in a dream, it is easy to free himself, to sit in judgment.

Will he really judge those people to death, have them handed over to the stubbly, sweaty soldiers? That child, isn't she at least too young? No, she's eight. She has reached the age of reason. A soldier drinks, and spits.

There is little sound, it is a very hot day, nothing stirs. In this sharp sunlight the fires will be almost invisible. There will be much dark smoke and the ashes will rise and rise.

But all this is better than doubt, they say.

But as he watches over this field of stakes with men, women, and children burning on them, like an orchard of dying manikins, the sirens start. Their long drawn-out up and down wail fills the streets, covers the field, rises up to the hills around the city. The gleaming missiles appear.

He wakes up. He feels himself filled with hopelessness, with an idea of this-cannot-be. He moves up to Diana, he presses his head against her shoulder, and he cries.

She doesn't completely wake up, she strokes his hair with her right hand. "Sh, sh," she whispers.

LXIV

Before going to work that morning he went to a house where a friend of his lived or used to live, with her boyfriend, a girl called Jinky. A decrepit brownstone in the East Thirties. He had left early and rang her doorbell at twenty minutes to nine.

It was Jinky who opened the door. She was in a housecoat, her hair in a scarf. It had been more than five years; she didn't look particularly pleased.

"Hello, Jinky. How are you? Sorry to bother you so early, but I couldn't get a phone number for you from information, I tried your name, and Charles's name." He spoke hurriedly as if afraid she'd close the door again.

"John. I've got to take the little girl to school. What's up?"

"Nothing, just that you still got a suitcase of mine in your basement, remember, from when I came to New York? I wonder if I could have a quick look, I need some papers."

"Oh. Oh yes. Come in." She stepped aside. "I have no time, can you help yourself? Pull the door closed when you leave, don't forget."

"Sure. Sorry to come at the wrong time."

She shrugged. "All times are wrong, it's hectic here. You know we had a flood last winter? It's all pretty much of a mess down there."

"I'll be careful. Are you okay? Is Charles okay?"

"Charles is okay," she said hastily. "We split, you know. He left, oh, three years ago. He's becoming the most famous black photographer in town, he's going to do a film next."

"No kidding. And you?"

"I—I have to get dressed. See you later maybe. You remember the way." She started back upstairs where a girl had been calling, "Mammy!" She stopped halfway up. "John—if you can take your things out of here, that would be nice. I don't have much space."

He went down the wooden stairs, more a ladder really, into the basement. Its floor was covered with dried mud and there was a chaos of tools and broken toys. He saw his suitcase in a corner covered with stacks of *New York Times* Sunday magazines. It was a big thing of beige imitation leather, he hadn't remembered it as so cheap looking. He didn't know any more what was in it, but surely no needed papers. He had suddenly thought of that suitcase in the night as an excuse for coming here.

It is the past. The past is security.

He stacked the magazines on the floor. Most of them toppled over. Never mind, I'll fix that later. The suitcase wasn't locked.

Books, mostly children's books which had been his. Empty picture frames. More *New York Times* magazines, for unknown reasons. Letters, he recognized his mother's writing, picture postcards she had always sent to him when she was away on some little trip. A scarf of hers and an old black leather wallet. The letter from Boston University accepting him. A bill from the hospital where his mother had died. School notebooks. Nice soft-cover ones without those damn spirals, you never see them nowadays, their pages empty.

He sat down on a stack of magazines and heard the child's high voice in the hallway, and the slamming of the front door. The lightbulb above his head flickered and went out. For perhaps five seconds he was lost then, unable to say where he was. The fear accompanying that was, miraculously, pleasurable. He sat in a dungeon and awaited the executioner. The House of Mercy.

The lightbulb flickered again. He stood up and touched it, it was loose. He put his handkerchief around one hand and screwed it tight, standing on tiptoe. With the light back on, he was unable to recall what he had just felt. He decided not to look any further, he carefully packed everything back into the suitcase. Two empty notebooks he kept out, but at the last moment he put those back in too. He piled the magazines on top. He carefully turned off the lamp.

It was then that he remembered Jinky's last words. He turned the light back on, put the magazines back on the floor, and dragged the suitcase up to the front door.

He started writing her a note but crumpled it up and put it in his pocket. That's a dead time. What am I doing here, waiting to shed a tear or two with her? She has more guts than I. And less time. Less time to be a slob. To search for security of old magazines in basements.

He pushed the suitcase out of the door and left it beside the garbage cans on the sidewalk.

LXV

A summons to Gene Oliver's office.

"You are seeing the personnel counselor," Oliver said.

"Ah—yes."

"He suggests you would profit from a rest period, an extended leave."

"I would not."

"Hold it a moment, Balthasar. Let me finish. He doesn't know and doesn't need to know that you're not on a regular contract, we've covered that ground before, remember. The thing is, it will have to be unpaid leave. Still, it seems unavoidable."

"I'm fine, Gene. As fine, that is, as anyone in this burg. And if I can't pay my rent, I'll be less fine."

"No, I must insist on a leave. I can't make any promises about what we'll do afterward, you know our budget problems. But we'll cross that bridge when we come to it."

Or jump in the river as the case may be. That fucker, realize your potential the man said. By getting kicked out. He hurried back to his room and phoned the Bellevue walk-in clinic. It was just after four. He didn't know the name of the counselor but when he mentioned the New York Public Library, a man came on and he recognized the voice.

"Yes, John, of course I remember. I've written you down for Monday the eleventh."

"To realize my potential. In the meantime you got me fired."

"I don't know what you're referring to, John. Calm yourself."

"I've just come from the head of administration here. Gene Oliver. He says you recommended a long rest period, as he put it."

"There's a misunderstanding somewhere, John. I haven't even seen you yet, how could I have done such a thing? We're professionals here."

Balthasar hung up, dialed Oliver. "Gene?"

A sigh. "Yes, Balthasar?"

"I just now talked to that counselor. On the telephone? He informs me that he did not recommend anything about me to anyone. Not a week's rest, not a year's rest, not an aspirin."

165

A silence.

"Gene? Mr Oliver?"

"I was gilding the lily for you, Balthasar. Sugar-coating the pill. The fact of the matter is, we've been advised that it would be in the interest of all concerned, you as well as us, if you, eh, kept to yourself for a while. Maybe stay with a friend or a relative, someone living in the country."

"Advised? Advised by whom?"

"An authoritative source."

"A what? By—by the goddamn FBI, right? I can't believe it! What the hell, it was me who went to see them! How dare they! How can you let them run the library for you! I can't believe it. I'm going to our director."

"If that's what you want, if you want to make yourself for ever impossible, I shan't stop you."

"How can you let them do it, tell you how to deal with your own people!"

"They're not. We discussed a situation, I accepted their advice."

"Oliver, listen, listen carefully. There is some very, very dirty business afoot. There's a conspiracy, terrible decisions, war, and they want us to shut up, stay out of it, they want to stop me from bugging them as if I were seeing little smurfs under my bed. I know—"

Oliver interrupted him. "You're overwrought. And you have been using the library time and the library telephone lines to call all over the place, to promote radical policies, in a word, to rabble-rouse. I don't know anything about a conspiracy, I don't know what you're about, and I don't want to know. This is a public institution with important benefactors. In matters of politics we keep a low profile."

"I've got a great suggestion for you, Oliver. Why don't you pack up this whole building, this whole temple of civilization, wrap up the ten million books, and shove not just the italic Dante, shove the whole outfit into a cave in the Rocky Mountains. You'll have the lowest profile anyone could hope for."

166

LXVI

He was leaning on the windowsill of a delicatessen near his bus stop and he had let a couple of buses go by. He couldn't bring himself to go home. He saw no way of telling Diana everything and did not know how to keep it hidden from her.

Harris and Oliver. Harris had tricked him, betrayed him. What could it mean but that they were in on this themselves?

Well, keep cool, it could just as well be that they considered him a pain in the neck, a crank, just that and nothing else. Was that likely? After that business with the classified-material forms?

A large number of men and women—

He tried to let his mind go blank. He turned and stared into the window of the shop, a man wiping the counter with slow, rhythmic movements, maybe he was singing a song to himself, an empty grill with a slowly turning spit. He straightened up, started walking toward Seventh Avenue.

He was going downtown instead of going home; he'd take the downtown bus, get off at Houston, and find his way back to that bar in the Bowery.

As a not totally desperate man might be moved by events toward a suicide he'd regret afterward if such were possible, thus Balthasar was drifting into the idea that he simply could not go home to his wife. He had to take flight and vanish. He had to protect Diana as long as possible by making sure she wouldn't have to lay eyes on him again. *Wife*—When I'm honest, when I peel off the make-believe, he thought, I know she is a stranger. The only thing we can share we have shared, we mixed our genes, she accepted that atom of sperm into herself. That is mine, but technically only, I have no knowledge of it, no sympathy with it, it does not perpetuate any Me. Still I must protect it.

Through no act of will he had come to think of the Bowery bar with the young whore in the blue raincoat who had told him she sat there every evening; he had seen that image of his, of the two of them walking toward a motel in the first light of day, in an unnamed small midwestern town, and he saw it as a projection of his future, his near future.

He didn't have the idea that it was a way to escape the great disaster; on the contrary. It was how to await it.

On that earlier night he had been on a Second Avenue bus which ended up in the Bowery. Now, riding down on the West Side and then crossing on Houston Street, it all looked different. He remembered the place so clearly, dark, the unlit wall lamps, the black and white television above a corner of the bar—I must find it.

He cut through a bit of Chinatown and then walked down empty streets where huge, silent trucks stood parked in long rows. The mechanics of daily life, the machine which is New York, continues turning quietly through the days and the nights. I wonder at what precise instant it will stop, at what exact second a cop writing a parking ticket will stop in the middle of a word and let his pad drop to the ground, in the atomic light.

Two bars, almost next to each other; he opened doors, pushed curtains aside, looked into faces turning toward him. No, neither of them.

A neon sign—that cleaner! He hurried to one corner, to another one; he had found his bar. It was exactly like last time, he sat down at the same table with a sense of painful familiarity. He thought he remembered each scratch and stain. He looked around: a couple of men. Tom behind the bar. I better have bourbon again, just for good luck.

"Isn't she here yet?" he asked the barman.

"Who is that?"

"Eh, Anna."

The man frowned. "I don't know any Anna."

Was that her name, had he just named her in his mind? "Young, thin sort of, dark-blue raincoat. She's got a fat woman in tow I think, that's her mother."

Tom frowned some more.

"But she's here every evening," Balthasar protested.

"Oh, that one." But Tom sounded as if he were just saying that to please his customer. "Yeah, hang around, maybe she'll show."

No, I know better. She will not show. She, like Andrea before her, is dead.

After that he did go home. He kissed Diana, she hadn't eaten yet, he cooked some spaghetti for her and himself. She seemed at peace with things, he thought. They talked little. He lay behind her in the night, pressing himself close to her in what they always called the spoon. He felt her warmth, her soft breathing. He fell asleep.

LXVII

He told Susan that he had been given sick leave. "I need an operation, nothing dramatic, something about a disk in my spine."

She looked up after turning a page in the manuscript in front of her. "I'm sorry. Take care of yourself."

"Will you be all right here alone?"

"They'd already warned me you might be away, and that someone from the Berg Collection could help out. It's not a busy time of year."

He was trying to guess what Gene Oliver might have told her, but she sounded as uninvolved and self-sufficient as always. "Maybe before I go, I'll clean out my desk anyway," he said.

She seemed genuinely surprised. "Why would you do a thing like that?"

"A doctor once told me, 'There's no such thing as a minor operation, there's always a chance you'll kick the bucket.'"

"He must have been a great comfort to his patients."

"Well, he didn't put it in those words, but that was the idea."

Balthasar had decided to leave during the lunch hour when few if any staff members were around. He hadn't been told he had to be out that same day but he wanted to avoid another meeting with Oliver at any price. He'd hit the man if he had to face him again. Sitting at his desk, he fitted his possessions into a cardboard box.

Never mind. None of this is very real. Shifting props between acts, fringe activities. Sediment. He looked in the box before closing it, it made him think of his mother's wallet, scarf, hospital bill in that old suitcase. But what about these, what about my Dante.

Five slim red and black volumes, still in need of rebinding. Not his Dante, the Library's Dante, but the idea of leaving them behind, of not seeing them again after that day at one o'clock, was intolerable. "I'll be damned if I leave them," he muttered.

Why not just put them in this box? No one knows I'm off for keeps, the guards know me, they're not going to embarrass themselves and me by checking.

Well, you never know. Wouldn't Oliver love to have me up for stealing from his collection.

Just then Susan walked around her desk, took her purse, and left the room with a little wave of her hand. That decided him. He pulled up his sweater and tried taping one of the volumes to his body. It worked. He did the same with the rest, making a circle of them around his middle, his sweater over it, his belt to keep them in place. His life preserver. He put his coat on, picked up his cardboard box, and left.

The guard at the public exit on Forty-Second Street did know him. "Hello John, what you got?"

"I'll be away for a couple of weeks, sick leave. Nothing dramatic, something about a disk in my spine. I'm taking some work home."

"Spines, they're a big nuisance, aren't they. My father-in-law has endless aggravation with that. You mind letting me have a look in the box? Rules, you know."

"Oh. Of course. Sure. Here you go."

"Okay, John. Take care now. Come back soon."

Balthasar stood in the street with his box. The tape pulled at his skin as he walked away. A very nice pain. He stopped at the newsstand and looked at the newspapers, at single words without trying to read the headlines, English, French, Hebrew.

But I'm acting as schizophrenic as those people I feel such contempt for, as Harris and Oliver.

He turned the corner to Fifth Avenue and sat down on the library steps, his box beside him. The sun was not out; it was a chilly, overcast day, but at that hour the steps were crowded anyway. He pulled his sweater up and peeled the little books off. A kid he had often seen there before, not older than fifteen or sixteen, a very ugly boy, was staring at him as he was doing that. He beckoned the boy over.

"Here," Balthasar said. "You want these? Don't ask why. They're worth a lot."

The boy did not answer.

"Well, they've got a bit of a history," Balthasar said with a meaningful smile. "You've got to be careful when you sell them. You know who'll take them, Dubner's, that place on West Twelfth Street. They're a messy place. Tell them you got them from your grandpa's library, he died of a coronary. Take them."

"Why? What're you up to?"

"Nothing, I'm tired of them. Take 'em." He put the books in the boy's hand, picked up his box and walked away.

As he waited for the light to cross Forty-Second Street, he looked back. The boy was standing next to a trash basket and as his eyes caught Balthasar's, he held each of the five volumes in turn at a corner, between thumb and forefinger, and then dropped it into the trash basket.

Balthasar watched this ceremony. Come corpo morte cade—as a dead man falling something something—

The light changed, he continued on his way.

LXVIII

That afternoon he became calm. He discovered he could keep himself going within an opaque vagueness. The following morning, his first day away from the library, he left the house at his normal hour. He wasn't ready to tackle the subject with Diana.

He sat with a cup of coffee in a drugstore and then took a subway downtown to the FBI. Harris wasn't there, they told him, and no, there was no one he could see without asking for an appointment in writing first. He became certain that the two men in the reception booth knew who he was, had been told on the phone to get rid of him. The lobby was crowded. He was tempted to stage a scene, get witnesses, *be a witness*, but he didn't. He shuffled away instead. He was indeed aware of his shuffling movements.

He telephoned Lucas and after many rings a recorded voice cut in to announce that the number had been disconnected. Then he tried Amparo. Just checking, he told himself, I'll call collect, if he accepts I'll hang up. But there he got the message, "The number is not listed at the request of the subscriber."

171

Now what. He took the uptown bus to Riverside Drive. As they passed Lucas's building, he saw men putting metal sheets in place on the ground floor windows. There were signs up, about relocation and that the place had been acquired by Thompson and Company. A De Luxe apartment building would be ready for occupancy in the spring of 1987. He did not get off the bus.

Have these men gone to ground? Gone to action-stations? Been locked up in Bellevue? Every cell in my body wishes me to shrug off this evil jumble and accept that they are crazy. Accept that I'm crazy. I'm not. It's true. It's true what Amparo told me.

He found himself walking east on 125th Street without remembering how he had got there. He entered another drugstore. A cup of coffee. He got up before the man had brought it and called Diana at her office.

"Hello, yes John?" she asked and in the words was so much warmth that he couldn't say what he had planned to say.

"I miss you," he answered. "Can I come over and take you to a posh lunch?"

"Can we afford it? It's a lovely idea."

With that, his life of a sudden was normal. Life became as it once was. A young couple, well, a young wife anyway, having a baby. Diana started talking about a whole string of subjects she had never brought up yet: which room was going to be the nursery; how the magazine was giving her a three months' leave of absence or even more if she needed it, but she thought she wanted to get back to work as early as possible; if they were careful they'd surely manage a daytime help or an au pair. He still didn't tell her anything about the library but his only thought about that was, to hell with 'em, there are other jobs.

He kept this up through the hours. It had become a warm afternoon. When he had walked her back, he wandered through the park and sat on the boathouse terrace. At five he went back to Diana's office to meet her. They cooked dinner together. She was tired and went to bed early. Tired but contented, she said.

When he woke up it was night. His watch had stopped at three o'clock. Or I am in dead time. It was very still in the apartment, not a sound rose from the street.

He lay motionless and then he felt drops of sweat starting to run down his cheeks. It was as if a curtain was raised within his mind. But I've been deluding myself, it is all as before. I cannot continue. I cannot possibly watch what will happen to Diana and to her baby.

That feeling started to fill him, filled him as water fills a vase. He began to tremble.

She is in labor when the explosion is heard—a rumble, as of thunder?—the flash. I can't see, she screams, my eyes, my eyes! the doctor and the nurse have run out of the room, her blood, bricks, plaster, the head of the baby—

Cautiously he got out of bed, opened the door slowly, went to the kitchen.

He turned the light on, he took a large kitchen knife out of the rack and looked at it.

I cannot, I need pills, the HCN scorpion. No, sleeping pills, they're gentle. A knife . . . I'm not very afraid of using it on myself, but I don't know enough. I don't know where to aim; it is unbearable if it is not instant for her. It is unbearable if she opens her eyes and looks at me.

He put the knife back in the rack. He heard a slight sound and saw her standing in the doorway, her eyes large and sleepy, childish eyes. "What you doing?" she whispered in a hoarse voice.

"Nothing. Nothing. I couldn't sleep—Let's go back to bed."

She let herself be led back to the bedroom, keeping her eyes closed. She immediately fell asleep again.

LXIX

Sun was shining through the room when they got up, sunlight reflected from windows across the street. "I'm late," she said while hurriedly getting dressed. She seemed to avoid really looking at him but he did not say anything about it. She drank some coffee standing at the sink and she left. "I'll talk to you on the phone," she called from the front door.

She knows. She's aware of what happened in the night. She is in fear of me now.

That evening—when? three, four days ago—I wasn't crazy, that

173

was the right impulse when I meant to vanish, take a bus to somewhere, anywhere. She is no longer safe with me.

For God's sake, who am I, how did I dare think of making myself master of her fate and of the fate of her child. I do not know anything, do I? Victim interfering with victim, pretending to be in control, to choose. Choice of death by gentle means. And how do I know even that, perhaps death with sleeping pills isn't remotely gentle, perhaps it's slow choking, a chemical garrote, with the, the heretic paralysed and unable physically to struggle but wanting to, desperately trying to.

How dare I think of such acts. Shy away from the executioners.

He telephoned after waiting one hour, then two hours.

"I didn't go to the library," he said.

"I realized." She sounded calm but tired. Sad perhaps.

"I'd better get out of here for some days, I figure. I'm in a state. Better for all of us, I mean. All three of us."

"Yes. Yes, John. You're right."

"Will you be okay by yourself?"

"Sure."

"I'll phone you."

A silence.

"Are you still there?" he asked.

"Listen." Her voice was lighter now. "Mother left me the keys to her house, she always does when she goes away. They're hanging in the kitchen, on the memo pad? Why don't you go there? There's no one, it will be very quiet."

"Eh—well, I—"

"It's a good idea," she told him. "It's lucky, her going to Chicago, I mean. She won't be back till the end of the month. If someone calls, just don't answer. And I'll know where you are. And you'll save a stack of money."

"Okay. Okay, I'll do that."

Am I being a coward now?

"You want me to call the library for you?" she asked. "What shall I say?"

"No, don't. I'll do it."

"I'll forward your mail. And the papers and everything."

"No!" he shouted. Then he laughed a little apologetic laugh. "I mean, don't. I'd rather not see anything. Unless there's something nice."

"All right, John. Only good news. And—"

"Yes?"

"And please let me tell Helfrich that you'll see him when you get back."

"Okay. Sure. I promise." He was about to ask her how to get to Northport, but then he asked instead, "What about your exercises? Don't you need me to take you to the Y?"

"That's all taken care of. One of the girls lives a minute away from us, on Central Park West. We had already arranged to go together from now on, I knew you hated those expeditions."

But I didn't. They were my best times. And he felt tears in his eyes, tears for himself.

He threw some things together into a zipper bag. Packing up once more.

LXX

In the subway station the woman selling tokens gave him directions which ended him up in Jamaica, Queens. A walk along endless blocks got him to a bus stop for Glen Cove. At least that was what a man in a flower shop told him. Others when asked looked away or incredulous.

When a bus arrived it was empty except for a black woman with many parcels and wearing large men's shoes. She listened in while Balthasar explained to the driver where Northport, his destination, was situated and vainly tried to elicit some comment from the man. She smiled at him, a fellow-victim smile, and he thought he should say something nice, but then she got off. The bus came to a turn-around and he had to get off too.

He started walking again. A terrifying landscape. Not because it was poor, it was not: there was a surfeit of machines; cars stood abandoned which in some parts of the world would have made their owners envied men or women. It seemed terrifying to him because it was a world hostile to itself, nomadic because it was destroying its last sources. The very names of the streets and roads were uncouth, names no child would want to remember as part of childhood, bestowed with terrible irony by public administrators with a premonition of the present.

Utopia Gardens.

He came to a bus shelter of shattered glass and prepared for a long wait. He had some forty dollars on him but the idea of taking a taxi did not enter his mind. After many changes of bus and much waiting and walking, he arrived at Northport.

It was now evening.

How odd, outlandish, to enter that empty house by himself. Echos from his wedding, from Easter Sunday. He did not look into any of the rooms. He closed those doors which stood open and went upstairs to a small guest room. It had blankets on its bed but no sheets; he drew the curtains, kept his underclothes on, swallowed some Valium which he had carried loose in his jacket pocket, and went to sleep.

LXXI

Time, days, now went by uncounted. As in Limbo.

He thought of calling Diana but was afraid to. Every now and again, rarely, Mrs Heffernan's telephone rang. The callers always tried for a long while. He did not answer and he went outside when the rings persisted.

Once he decided to walk to the shore of the Sound but after a few minutes he came to a fork. He had forgotten the way, and he turned back.

There were huge supplies of food in a freezer and he ate bits and pieces, strange combinations.

Then, at twilight, sitting in the kitchen, he saw a red light streaking and flashing around the walls of the room. It did not frighten him. It startled him and gave him a sense of relief, of easing. The fog would lift, something was happening. The bell rang loudly, twice, and he went to open the door.

A police car, two troopers looking at him. He looked at himself, with them: he was unshaven, dressed in trousers and an old windbreaker he had found on a nail in the kitchen.

"We got some calls," one of the men said. "We're just checking. You a house sitter?"

"Yes, sort of."

"Friend of Mrs Pollack, are you?"

"Pollack? Mrs Heffernan lives here. I'm her son-in-law."

The man grinned. "Just checking, sir. That's all right then."

"You okay here?" the other policeman asked.

"Sure. I'm okay."

"The news is sure something," the other man now said conversationally.

"The news? What is—?" Balthasar began but then he said, "Yeah, it's sure terrible."

"Oh I dunno," the first man said. "It's good they see they can't push us around."

"Yeah."

"Well, good night, sir. Sorry for the interruption."

"Good night, officers."

LXXII

He remained standing in the doorway, looking after the police car. Once its revolving light had vanished behind the hedge and his eyes had become used to the dark, he saw a star, one, then several, in the gaps between the clouds in the black sky. Star light star bright first star I see tonight wish I may wish I might grant this wish I wish tonight. Or something like that.

Preserve us.

He went back indoors and now for the first time walked through all the rooms. There was only one television set in the house, a large one in the living room. He unplugged it and carried it into the hallway where he shoved it into a closet. He locked the closet and at the front door he threw out the key in a wide arc. It landed soundlessly in the grass.

I will stay up tonight, he decided. I must conduct a vigil. I will try and watch over Diana at least.

He had seen a box of candles in the kitchen and he now lit some, putting them in a circle around the room. He turned off the

177

electricity at the main switch and heard the hum in his head of the total silence when the motors of the freezer and the refrigerator stopped.

He sat on a kitchen chair, the candles around him, and asked himself what a prayer could mean in this condition, in this year of human history, in this last hour of the Quaternary Period. Imagine, try to think of a man, a Neanderthal man or whatever he was called, praying to God or just to a tree or a mountain, after all those billions of years but still, that was our dawn. And now, is it over?

I wish I had studied geology. There must be immense consolation in that. If we survive I'm going to study geology. Somehow. With a job on the side, anything. Tie myself to the structure of universe time.

LXXIII

He slept a fitful sleep in which thoughts and pictures seemed to pass through his mind as if for inspection.

He got to his feet at the very first glimmer of day, in the false dawn as they had told him in high school that sailors call it, at the moment when a black and a white thread can be distinguished from one another, as an Egyptian had told him Moslems define it.

The candles were burned out. He didn't turn the lights back on as he made his way to the kitchen tap, hitting himself on the edge of the table. Black and white thread. He thought about that; it was a holy moment of some kind.

The hallway was cold and he put on a sheepskin jacket he saw on the clothes stand. He left the house. He didn't know where the keys had gone and left the front door unlocked.

This time he went past the fork in the road, and he reached the shore, faster than he had expected. The Sound lay unruffled, gray; seagulls were riding it, sleeping on the water. Misty as during the evening of his wedding, and the lights of the Connecticut shore blinking through it. He wandered down a winding road until a gate stopped him. There was a notice board but the light was still too dim for him to read it. He tried to sit on the gate. The wood was sharp. Then he just stood there.

This world. We aren't in a Greek tragedy or in an opera. It is all happenstance, little figures on an endless stage who try to move settings and backdrops which reach beyond the stars. But there is happiness all the same, there was happiness. Times of excitement, of love, music, a young girl on a bicycle singing, Oh Baby Baby, it's a Wild World. Perhaps pity is the cue and the last key. Perhaps those gray men truly believed that the screams and the burning bodies of the auto-da-fé pleased their God.

Miguel. Surviving all those years, that war of his, to end up in the back seat of an abandoned car beside a grimy canal. And I, well, Jesus Christ, I wasn't even interested in Spain ever, it was that damn *Penthouse* assignment. I never liked that manliness bullfighter hokum. Even as a boy I didn't like Hemingway. I could walk back to the house now and put in a call to that Huelca policeman. What's police again in Spanish? He tried to conjure up the word as it appeared on the police cars but he could not get it clear. Or maybe they were the Guardia Civil? What difference could it make? What could one say?

It's midnight or something there now.

But I'm pleased now for that kid with the big head on the library steps, that he threw my Dante into a trash can. What had I been thinking, what was that enthusiasm of mine about? Jealousy. I must have been dizzy with jealousy about that peak of peace, of reason, of sense, of eternity four-thousand-years-long. A lovely neatness as in a boarding school, as in a family.

I wonder what became of my father, if my life would have been different if.

He saw himself as a boy, walking with his mother. Where? A town square, a photographer used to sit there near the fountain, with a camera on a tripod, they had their picture taken once. That must have been when he was very young. Really, a camera on a tripod? The picture hadn't been in his mother's possessions, had she sent it off to someone? To his father even?

Then he thought of his own child, not yet born, of holding her hand, his hand. He was confused, he was the child too. Darkness.

179

LXXIV

He started back to the house. Nothing stirred, he met no one. A high note from a bird, a single one, stopping almost the instant it started. As if surprised.

When he walked up the driveway of the house, he noticed the mailbox, on a pole at the end of the lawn. He hadn't been aware of it before. A hunting dog was painted on it, just visible now, with a duck flying above its head. He took out the fat bundle of mail. It felt soggy; it would have been there a long time.

In the hesitant early light he could make out most of the addresses. A few letters to Mrs Heffernan, the rest advertisements and printed things.

A letter to him from Diana.

He took out the note and tried to read it. But then he stopped himself, his hands shook and he dropped it to the ground.

Flies. He had dreamt of flies that night, and the night before, and now he remembered. After the bombs there were new species of flies, huge, five inches long, mutants, because there was so much food for them in all the streets, in all the houses. Large green-shimmering flies, unthreatened for there were no more birds. I must beat them to it. I want a grave, with flowers, if only for a year, if only for a week.

He picked Diana's note up from the ground, it was muddy but he put it back into the envelope. The postmark was smudged, illegible. He put the letter and the rest of the mail carefully back into the mailbox. He went in and dialed her number. Our number, briefly.

The telephone rang a long time. She's left, she is coming here. No, she would—"Hello?" her voice, sleepy and tired.

"I'm sorry, I'm sorry," he said. "I'm waking you. But your letter. . . ."

"Oh John. That's all right. I'm very glad. Of course you called. Are you, are you cheering up a bit out there?"

"Absolutely."

"It's pretty countryside, isn't it?"

"Yes."

"I've been okay here," she said.

180

"Diana—no messages?"

"Eh, no. What are you expecting?"

"Nothing, nothing. Go back to sleep. I'm sorry. I didn't realize how early it is."

"I *am* tired. Let me call you back in an hour or so, all right, John?"

"Yes. Do that. There wasn't any card?"

"What? Call after eight, and I'll be bright-eyed and bushy-tailed."

"No card?"

"Card . . . well, no . . . ads, bills."

"A card with a cross and a Latin inscription, like that Lucas seal, remember?"

"Lucas seal?"

Don't repeat everything, he said soundlessly through his teeth. "Exsurge Domine et judica causam tuam," he shouted. Or thought he shouted.

A silence.

"Diana, are you still there?"

"Eh, something like that did come, perhaps," she murmured. "Maybe . . . I must have thrown it away. No, that was an ad. . . ."

"What? Are you sure?"

"Yes, John. John, I've got to get some more sleep now or I'll be dead on my feet all day. Call me after eight, okay? You need that card? I'll look in the trash can, maybe it's still—eight, okay?"

"Okay."

"Darling," he said. "Go back to sleep." But there was no more answer. She had already hung up, perhaps.

He was certain now that time had almost run out.

He turned back the way he had gone before, back to the water. But now he pushed the gate until it opened, he crossed the parking lot of a yachting club, came to a wall he climbed over. Cinders and then the water's edge.

He sat down on a flat rock. The little waves just touched his shoes.

In the east the sky had a pink band along the horizon. Above that it was green, a pure, spring green.

In the west above New York the clouds were rosy. They were lit from below by the million lights of the city. Those clouds were low and dark-topped.

The flashes will be within the clouds, and bursting through them. Like sunrays. Like the rays in one of those Rembrandt skies. The connotation made him almost smile. Very civilized.

I did not fight, I did not have to be held down as I had promised. The executioner is beyond my reach. We are wearing the yellow robes already.

Then all he was aware of was the hammering of his heart. There were no possible thoughts left.

He would not avert his eyes, on the contrary.

He waited there, sitting very still.

Hans Koning was born Hans Koningsberger in Holland. He was still in school when the Germans invaded; escaping to England, he came to this country via wartime service in the British Army and a year as a radio producer in Indonesia. In 1958 his first novel, *The Affair*, set his reputation as an American writer. He has published ten more novels, among them *An American Romance*, *A Walk with Love and Death*, *The Petersburg-Cannes Express*, and *Death of a Schoolboy*. Some of these were made into motion pictures. He has also been a reporter at large for *The New Yorker*, which led to such nonfiction books as *Love and Hate in China* and *A New Yorker in Egypt*.

He changed his name to Koning in 1972, five years after becoming one of the founders, with Noam Chomsky, of the antiwar group Resist in Cambridge, Massachusetts, and during the Vietnam years most of his work was devoted to the movement. (The mood of the time is recalled in his recently published book, *Nineteen Sixty-Eight, a Personal Report*.) Toward the end of the Vietnam War, he moved temporarily to England in what he called a self-imposed exile, and while there he worked for the Campaign for Nuclear Disarmament. Elements from these years come together in *Acts of Faith*.